THE
STAKED
PLAINS

Also by Stefan Kiesbye

Next Door Lived A Girl

Your House is on Fire, Your Children All Gone

Messer, Gabel, Schere, Licht

Fluchtpunkt Los Angeles

The Staked Plains

S TEFAN K IESBYE

Saddle Road Press

Saddle Road Press
Hilo, Hawai'i
www.saddleroadpress.com

Cover photo and book design: Don Mitchell
Goathead images: Betty Williamson
Author photo: Sanaz Kiesbye

ISBN 9780991395279
Library of Congress Control Number: 2015951477

For Sanaz

Contents

ONE

Then said I, O my lord, what are these? And the angel that talked with me said unto me, I will shew thee what these be.

SHE WAS A BAD PSYCHIC when she arrived in Querosa, New Mexico, not because she didn't possess the powers, but she couldn't control them. Her husband moved them to the small town to teach at the college and she didn't have anything to persuade him not to. "We'll make it fun," he promised, and after thirty days on the High Plains, the Great Drought began. People seemed friendly.

In Los Angeles Jenny had dealt with all sorts of clients. In her first few months in Querosa she encountered only three—people who wanted to believe in God and still wanted to make sure; women who wanted to know how much longer they had to endure their husbands; and dairy cowboys in soiled jeans and boots who didn't want anything they could articulate but who came nonetheless. They expected crystal balls and tea leaves, but all they had to do was take off their boots and socks. Sometimes Jenny read hands, but it was looking at their feet that told her most about the people coming to her small place on Avenue D.

Her hair was strawberry blond, her complexion of a near yellowish white, and freckles abounded. How could they not? Jenny liked to joke that when it came to all things magic, you could do worse than having long, red hair. She said her boobs helped too, they kept shy men coming.

She might have been Irish but wasn't, and there were rumors spread carefully throughout her family's history that her great-great-great-grandmother had been a witch from the Black Forest who'd barely escaped Germany to the New World. Jenny was rather fond of that cobwebbed tale, mended by each generation of women. They kept it intact, even though their last names changed and tore the women apart. Grandma Vollmer, the witch was called, and Jenny had been born a Kestendorf and quite gladly switched to Preston.

Carl Preston, her husband, was easy to live with, a big man of great enthusiasm, which he bestowed on most everything. On his job as an anthropologist at the small, regional university, on their new house, their first, and on the plants and the lawn which were always close to death from the 100-degree heat, and on Jenny. He had an enthusiasm for her body, which turned him as loud and awkward as a Great Dane spotting a cat, and his good-natured assaults on her were a series of grunts and thrusts and yelps and brief barks. Then he leapt up to devote himself to work or garden and left her bruised and listening to his sounds around the house or in front of her window.

They'd been married for seven years. He hadn't slowed down.

On the fields just north of their house, on a street named after a state she would have willingly offered to Mexico or Canada or used as a fenced-in asylum for anti-abortionists, Limbaugh lovers, and the entire Bush administration, cows grazed, dust was lifted into the air and dropped onto their windowsills. On many days it smelled as though she were rubbing her nose in their two dogs' nether regions, but Carl hardly noticed. In his air-conditioned office in one of the nicer campus buildings, he noticed little about Querosa. His truck displayed the slogan 'Pray for Rain,' as though he belonged here, and yet he didn't know Taco Town, the other side of the railroad tracks, where migrant workers and poor farmhands lived. Mostly Mexicans, legal and illegal alike.

He didn't know about the gun raffle at Leighton's Feed Store. Carl didn't know how often the freight trains came through town or that there hadn't been a passenger train in forty years and that the old train station was for sale and would have made for a nice restaurant and bar, if someone had had the eye to see its potential. But in a town of barely 10,000, who would have eye and money?

The ethanol plant and the peanut plant opened and closed their doors, fired and rehired workers constantly. More people seemed to be out of work than have a steady job.

Carl knew campus, and his enthusiasm for work and home blinded him. Jenny knew the German word for her husband: *kindskopf.* Carl, the *kindskopf.* She loved his childlike demeanor —she'd been attracted to his boisterous self that seemed to plough through problems as though they were as immaterial as the first snow at the end of November.

At night she woke sometimes, assured by his loud breathing and wished for more. More darkness maybe, more dangerous undercurrents, treacherous depths. Anything that might scare her. She wanted a sharper pain.

In Los Angeles, where Carl had finished his degree at UCLA, she'd first worked out of the dining area of their one-bedroom apartment. Friends of friends had arrived and she'd read them their fortunes. Jenny had tried to read tea leaves and coffee grounds and hands. She liked hands well enough, the wear and tear that chronicled a life better than faces could, especially in LA where faces were something you aspired to. Yes, it was a cliché, the old, so old LA cliché, and yet Jenny had admired the discipline with which actors and doctors and lawyers and people with the time and the money kept their faces in check. She understood the art behind the smooth, taut features.

Yes, she'd liked hands, but she'd found her opening to character and future in feet. This was hard to admit, and harder to tell her clients. People trusted her with their hands but they felt silly and naked when Jenny took their feet in her lap and stared at bunions, neglected nails, squeezed toes. And the carefully manicured feet were no different. Shy and awkward, children hidden away in closets, blinded by the attention. Still.

The lint between toes, the shape of the big toe, the length of toes—it was there that Jenny saw futures. Maybe it was a result of the clients' reluctance, their smiles of disbelief, their horror at taking off their shoes that made her grasp the person.

LA had been easy—many of her customers had been raised in flip-flops, but Querosa was another matter. The very first person to come through the door of the compact stand-alone building on Avenue D seated himself at the small, round table and when Jenny asked the 50-year-old to remove his heavy boots he grinned, shook his head, whistled, and walked away. The sticker on his truck endorsed the GOP in no uncertain terms. In Querosa that didn't mean much. God was spelled GOP.

No matter how her day went, she made sure to take what she called her sanity-break. She couldn't stay six or eight hours in her office without going home and returning to herself. On bad days that meant eating way too much for lunch without even looking at the food. On good ones, she just wandered through her house, that modest brick ranch, or sat in the sunroom with some tea and a magazine. She fed Xerxes and Shibuya, her dogs, watched them sun themselves in the yard. Her breaks rarely lasted longer than an hour. She didn't need rest, she needed to remember and recognize her life again.

The first customer who stayed was also a man, younger, though not young. He wore a flannel shirt and a white cowboy hat, called Jenny *Ma'am* and pulled off his boot without a second of hesitation. "She's not sure," he said, as though this explained why he'd come.

"You want her to be?" Jenny asked. She'd chosen a thin sweater to wear, with a nice neckline, a soft bra that outlined her breasts. She wore jeans and simple mules. She didn't want to read other people's lives with bare feet.

Her red hair she wore open and the simple outfit was designed to put customers at ease. In LA she'd worn more colors, more make-up. LA was fickle. Here, the only hint at what she did were turquoise earrings and a matching necklace. Everything else was a matter of lighting.

"I'll marry her if she is," he said.

"But you don't want to?"

"I don't?"

Jenny smiled, put his right foot in her lap, with care, not tenderness. It was a white foot with dirty nails, a steady foot with a good-enough arch, a bit rigid though. She looked at and felt it. She noticed the very dark hairs growing on the man's toes.

"She's not for you," she said after a few minutes. "And she's not pregnant. But if you go back to her she will be. Soon." She exhaled. "What does your wife know about this? She doesn't yet, right? But she's on to you. This is the first time you strayed. You like your wife better, but..." She stopped. There seemed to be a knot in her thoughts, as though the foot in front of her had produced it. "She's older, no, no, but she is..." She let go of the man's foot. It fell to the floor like a dropped cup, only it didn't shatter.

He didn't seem to mind, his eyes hung on Jenny.

"You must leave her," she said before she could stop herself.

"Why? She's my wife," the man said. "So I should go with..."

"Just leave. Leave your family. You're living in a trailer next to your parents' house. Leave, go, just get out of there, get out of this town."

"Now you're talking crazy shit," the man laughed. He was 39 maybe, 38. He put on his boot and took the agreed-upon twenty from a stitched leather wallet. "She's my wife."

"You would have left her for your girlfriend."

"Yeah, but she's no good, right?"

"She's not pregnant, she's not in your future."

"Thanks, ma'am," he said, and his grin was not so different now from that of her first visitor. "We grow green chile, it's the family tradition. We're a great family. I'm needed."

Jenny nodded. The man stood up, waited for a last word from her, and she forced herself to say, "You take care now," and then failed to see him walk out to the parking lot, failed to listen to his truck's mangled exhaust pipe.

What she saw was his wife in his older brother's bed, and the child she would soon carry, and she saw the man's path forking and also knew that he would take the one that would lead him back to his family and some future event that felt like bile shooting up her throat and she opened her eyes wide to let her surroundings convince her that she was still in her office and only when she stopped did she notice she'd been crying. She didn't have another customer that day.

Two

And there appeared a great wonder in heaven; a woman clothed with the sun, and the moon under her feet, and upon her head a crown of twelve stars: And she being with child cried, travailing in birth, and pained to be delivered. And there appeared another wonder in heaven; and behold a great red dragon, having seven heads and ten horns, and seven crowns upon his heads. And his tail drew the third part of the stars of heaven, and did cast them to the earth: and the dragon stood before the woman which was ready to be delivered, for to devour her child as soon as it was born.

SHE COULD RECOGNIZE A TOWN by the way it kept its dogs, and Jenny's stomach had turned sour that first afternoon they drove into Querosa. Mangy pit bulls stood in piles of trash, mutts were chained to poles and fences in 100-degree heat. In Querosa, there was no shade. There were no mountains, no hills, there was no river. These were the Eastern High Plains, the Staked Plains, and the joke Jenny heard more than once during her first months was that if your dog ran away, you could see him run for three straight days.

Querosa claimed to have 17,000 people, but 6,000 of them were students at the college, and during the summer they left. The courthouse was the most prominent building, a bland art deco block set in the middle of what was now a large parking lot. This was the main square and around its edges, a consignment store, a fitness center, and a saddle maker hung on for dear life. There was an Italian restaurant and a coffee and sandwich shop. There was the post office. The Chamber of Commerce. Two insurance agents.

Farther down the road, on the way out of town, was the best Mexican restaurant, set in a tire shop. Carl and Jenny got their tires rotated while eating huevos rancheros, and the waitress rang them up for both.

Querosa had a donut shop, a steakhouse, a diner, a local taco chain and a local fast food joint. McDonald's outdid Burger King. You could join a Christian fitness club and get Christian massages. It had two Christian barber shops, and a Christian Motorcycle Club. Querosa had 62 churches.

The tap water turned children's teeth brown, Jenny had been told, and everyone she knew got their drinking water from a purifying station in town. It was cheap and didn't smell. The smell of the tap water was intermittent and nauseating, as if it came directly from the ground beneath the dairy farms surrounding the town. The wind carried their sickening smell into the streets and into the houses. Querosa had no rain, but it had enough wind. It hardly ever let up.

The best coffee available in Querosa was McCafé. Carl refused to go, refused also to stop at Walmart, but Jenny was more pragmatic. That afternoon, she didn't drink her latté, just held on to it. She'd been in trouble before with clients who needed saving and she wanted to be the one who pulled them out of a roiling sea into the lifeboat, and yet she'd learned that this couldn't, mustn't, be her role. She was a discloser, not a guide. She mustn't make decisions for the futures she saw but could not completely grasp. She could point out the cliffs, the rocks, reefs, and undercurrents, but if she tried to keep people from drowning, they'd pull her with them to the bottom.

It had happened before. A customer, a woman in her late twenties, had gotten so enraged at Jenny's pleas to leave her lover, that she pulled a gun from her Bottega Veneta bag. She hadn't fired it, but she had died in her lover's car that night, apparently after a fight. He'd lost control, and the occupants of the oncoming car had died as well.

She hadn't talked to Carl about it, because he looked at her psychic abilities the way a parent might look at his small daughter's hands smeared with chocolate and dirt.

The question she asked herself was simple and therefore had no answer. Had she seen the accident or produced it?

Jenny had resumed her readings a week later, but she didn't give advice anymore. She had breached her own rules with that man in his cowboy boots, and she hoped there'd be no fallout. Just because he had never been to LA or New York or Europe didn't mean she could repeat past mistakes. She hoped she'd never see him again. Or if she saw him, it wouldn't be in the back of a police car.

Then one day a man brought three children to the McDonald's. He had black hair and a short, black beard. He looked pleasant enough. 'Coach' was printed in caps on the back of his shirt and he didn't sit down with the two boys, seven and ten maybe, but next to the teenage girl, who had 'Champions 2' printed on her shirt. They moved in too close to one another. Jenny saw with sudden clarity that the girl was the man's daughter and more, much more, and she changed seats. It wasn't her life to live, she had a coffee to nurse.

The next moment she turned abruptly. What was her gift worth if she didn't act on it? Yet her wish to help was hubris, some voice inside her head assured her. She looked at people's lives and gave them choices; it wasn't her place to interfere. She stared at the girl's black hair, stacked on her head like a resting cat, watched her lean into the man, saw him respond in kind, and fled the restaurant. Choices. It didn't have to come to this.

Jealousy was a strong motivator, so were thoughts about future families, and always health and wealth. Office traffic was sparse. This was not LA, where money had to be spent on German cars, manicures, shrinks, and psychics. A few of Jenny's visitors were college students who had fallen in love and were thinking about marriage and who stuck their feet in her lap as though they were pigs' hooves. They were grossed-out by themselves, they had cuts on their thighs and a vague interest in puppies and babies. They couldn't remember the faces of their fiancés, just their hair and crotch smells , which were always objectionable.

A few stiff-limbed women who still dreamed of the antebellum South and carried it like broomsticks in their torsos sat down to talk about savings, strangers they wished and were afraid to meet, and the afterlife. Their very white, brittle feet seemed shrunk, like dried fish, dehydrated like the earth in the savage Querosa heat, and they said, "I can't talk to him?"

And Jenny shook her head, held on to feet, and said, "I'm here for the living."

"They say the drought will continue," one of them, who introduced herself as Delores Price, said so quietly and without expression that Jenny immediately knew that she had to be on her guard.

"It's what they say," Jenny answered in the same tone of voice.

Mrs. Price stared at her. "What do you want me to do?"

Jenny smiled and soaked up the stare until the woman finally blinked and pulled off her sandals. The polish was chipped, the nails thick and yellow underneath.

"The Lord gave you powers," she said.

Jenny didn't answer, received the right foot and warmed it in her hands. It was as dry as sandpaper. "Is there anything you'd like to know?"

"Or it was the devil who did."

"You've never been married."

"Everybody knows that," Price sneered.

"Because the man you wanted was taken."

Price narrowed her eyes. "They talk about you."

"Of course," Jenny said.

"Some say you shouldn't have been allowed to open this..." she looked around, "...parlor."

"He didn't want you, though," Jenny said without changing her voice. "He had other plans."

The old woman pulled her foot away. "Gossip. We don't need some stranger rummaging through our drawers. Who told you?"

"The devil?" Jenny said.

To her surprise, the foot returned.

"They say you can put a hex on people," Price said without looking at Jenny. The small refrigerator in the back of the building started up with a clatter.

It was Jenny who released the foot and put it gently on the floor. "They are mistaken," she said.

"They are? You are a disappointment, dear." Her foot fished blindly for its shoe. "Are you here to buy up land? To get rich?"

"Is the land worth anything?"

"Not at this moment. But that can change quickly. Haven't you seen the expensive cars on the square and in front of the Italian restaurant? California license plates. They're not here to talk cattle and peanuts."

"What else?"

Price narrowed her eyes once more. "Really? Are you that naïve? Isn't your husband a professor at the college? Ask him. We're all going to swim in it."

Jenny said nothing. Price's foot hadn't told her anything, it had been dead weight in her hands. A cut of beef. She had heard rumors about Price and her one-time liaison with a certain J.D. Hartt, a banker. How his parents had forced him to abandon the woman who was ten years his senior for a more suitable candidate. She carried the broken promise with her like an old purse; it was meticulously cared for, and bright green and obvious.

"I won't come back," Price announced.

"And you don't owe me anything," Jenny said when the woman opened her wallet.

"But when I do, we're going to drive your ass out of town. Yes, we will." Then she smiled, shook her gray hair and walked out the door. Jenny watched her cross the parking lot, watched the gait of her new foe, the eagerness of every step.

Delores Price looked like an excited choirgirl or a young nun in love with Jesus Christ

Across the street from her salon, a massage studio opened its doors. The day before it had been an abandoned building, now a large poster hung above the entrance. Behind the window, a big LED sign promised foot massages. Yet the parking lot in front of the darkened store windows remained empty. Once or twice a day a woman in cut-off jean shorts and flip-flops stood by the door and smoked a cigarette. She looked Asian, might have been in her mid or late thirties. Who would her clients be? Who in Querosa had money for massages?

The next day Jenny had trouble extracting a padded manila envelope from the mailbox she had painted silver and red. It was addressed to Professor H. Darling, a name she'd never heard mentioned, and had been sent by a Dr. Finis Joyce from Missouri. It wasn't her mail, the address wasn't even the right one, but she tore it open anyway, simply because she could feel the book stirring inside the envelope, like a baby.

But what a disappointment. *What the Bible Has to Say About Angels* was the clumsy title. Finis Joyce had authored it.

"Angels?" Jenny asked out loud while looking at their neighbor across the street, the Calvary Baptist Church. "Angels?"

Joyce asked Darling for advice on his writing, though Jenny thought it strange to ask someone for advice after finishing and publishing the book. What good could any advice be now? Dr. Joyce had been "blessed" with six children, according to the back cover. Advice on raising them would have been equally moot. She hoped they had turned out better than this badly printed and bound book.

Most of the university students were poor, many of them working long hours in fast food joints and at Walmart. Some were military, Air Force men and women from the nearby base, which specialized in drone programs. At night you could sometimes hear the drones, neighbors swore. They were prototypes, with capabilities beyond those you heard about on TV. They could listen in on any conversation, they could detect anybody hiding inside buildings. They could spray chemicals onto lawns and through windows. Many people in town were sick, these people said, and could you be sure allergies were to blame. Allergies in the desert?

Carl had been a promising grad student, and at night, over wine or vodka, he now said, "I was lucky to even land a job." Others in his cohort were still adjuncting or had already left the field. Querosa had been his sole campus interview and he had joked that he was too overqualified not to get the position. You came to Querosa when you didn't have a choice.

Eastern Plains University was a third-tier institution where Carl's efforts at finishing his book about the Hohokam and the Hemenway expedition were silently discouraged. Small frowns, blank stares, tiny disgusted sighs let him know he was too ambitious. 'Student Success Is What We're All About' was Eastern Plains' motto. *The Old New World: Hemenway's Southwestern Archaeological Expedition in 1887-88,* which did not contribute to successful student outcomes, remained a first draft. Carl had not even contacted a publisher.

One night, Jenny suggested a walk, which soon ended at the fence overlooking a field and a smattering of cows. A nearby dumpster hummed with flies.

Carl bent her over, his preferred position, and she was in the mood and chose to watch the cows while feeling Carl going at it as though he were in a hurry. He probably was. And she liked his urgency, he knew what he wanted and how he wanted it and before long he walked off, zipping himself, not bothering to caress her or shield her buttocks from possible view. "You coming?" he asked. There was no malice in him. He just wasn't there. Perhaps he was afraid he might disappear if he ever touched down, if he stayed with her a bit longer. Jenny lowered her dress and stood up. A white-faced cow eyed her with interest.

Three

Neither can they die any more: for they are equal unto the angels; and are the children of God, being the children of the resurrection.

IN THE MORNINGS, before she drove to her small office, she sometimes stopped at Higher Grounds, the only coffee shop in town, one the college students ignored and only the lunch crowd found appealing. The coffee was mediocre, but at least the beeps and whirs of the McDonald's were absent.

Every day, a roundtable of middle-aged-and-beyond men congregated here, and she felt their gazes clinging to her dress like goatheads, while the barista, the owner's son, walked flat-footed to the refrigerator to retrieve the two-percent milk for her latté.

"Who are they?" she asked the kid, bestowing a smile on him she hoped was inviting and disarming enough for him to lower his voice and lean toward her for an answer.

He followed her train of thought and said, "J.D. Hartt, he owns this building, and the others on the square. And the bank, of course." He stopped for a second, then added, "You don't get anything here if he doesn't want you to. Sugar-free vanilla?" he asked in a slightly louder voice.

She nodded, waited several beats before glancing back at the table, and she knew immediately who Hartt was. He wasn't the most imposing man, probably not much taller than herself, and he wasn't the loudest one either, but all the other men's faces pointed like bright-red arrows at his. Jenny could feel the discomfort they felt. They were on their guard, and they chose their words carefully. He was the only man at the table who seemed relaxed and to be enjoying himself. The only one whose laughter went on for too long.

His receding hair was a touch wavy, gray, and he wore a Tom Selleck mustache. He had been young in the 70s, now his belly made him sit back from the table. He wore a flannel shirt, a large belt buckle in silver and gold. His jeans were none too clean. And while she was still studying him, he looked over without a smile. He just stared, then finally nodded.

Over coffee, she read magazines she'd recently subscribed to. *Entertainment Weekly*, *Yoga*, *Granta*, *Harper's*, *Harper's Bazaar*, *ArtNews*, *JuxtaPoz*, *Elle*. She didn't like them all, but without them she felt she was dying. Querosa had a newspaper with twelve pages daily and most of the content was religious, right wing, or plain drivel. None of it was grammatical.

The Albuquerque paper was not available, the *New York Times* did not deliver. The Internet was no alternative for Jenny. She needed coffee stains. She read papers and magazines three times a day. After breakfast, for lunch, and later maybe in the bathroom. She got a lot of use out of one paper.

He didn't come to her table that day. J.D. Hartt left without her noticing. Only after the men filed out of the coffee shop did she catch one last glance of his pot-bellied, very erect figure. He could have been Hollywood thirty years ago.

The drought forced people to sell their cattle. The drought drove others off their land. The Eastern Plains' campus, in the summer the only oasis of green, was dying—the city had capped its water supply, there was nothing left for plants. Trees were dying by mid-June and the wind blew up great clouds of dust. Even at night, the temperature did not sink below eighty.

The town's stray dogs began to die. One morning, Jenny found a pit bull in her driveway, his eyes still open. He had no collar, his white fur was yellow and brown from the dust. He didn't seem hurt, nothing seemed broken. She loaded the dog into the back of her station wagon and drove out to the state park and buried him close to a deserted campsite. It was the wrong thing to do, and yet nothing better came to her mind.

The moment she stowed the shovel in her car, she went rigid. This was the first time she felt the pain. Somewhere below the navel yet far away from the surface. If she had been traveling, she would have suggested constipation. She put a hand on the back door and slowly stood. She was quickly drenched in sweat.

Carl was away for a few days on a dig—observing, studying with a colleague near Santa Fé. She had looked forward to an empty house but after a day it already felt too large and unwieldy. Her clothes, magazines, and coffee mugs littered the place and begged for attention. She couldn't fall asleep without Carl's big, noisy breathing, without his weight next to her. The Monsoon season had brought no rain.

Sometimes, when she got up early enough to catch the pre-ninety-degree heat, she put on old running shoes, leashed her dogs, and ran with them past her street into the fields, past the Baptist children's home, past some dilapidated trailers that housed families and unchained dogs who followed her with threatening barks. Her dogs, Xerxes and Shibuya, strained and bared their teeth. Xerxes, a twelve-year-old Husky, growled, but Shibuya was beside her, getting up on two legs, begging to be let off her leash. After the first such episodes, Jenny packed Graham crackers and threw them at the trailer dogs and they left her alone.

After another two miles, a set of abandoned trailers appeared on her right. The wind had carried off any truck or car tracks, the windows were broken, the roofs had been partly peeled off. The trash had stuck around though, clinging to every bush and tree. Plastic bags, a child's tricycle, a carcass that might have been a cat or a dog.

Jenny stopped to catch her breath, taking in the meanness of the place, and yet she couldn't bring herself to hate it. She named it Yucca Lows because everything around here was called Yucca-something or other. Plumbers, phone and car companies; she lived in the neighborhood of Yucca Heights—a silly name since the Heights were just a few feet above the town's general 4,000 foot level. Just above flood level, though no one remembered the last flood brought on by torrential rains.

The abandoned trailers were the Lows. That they were allowed to exist soothed Jenny like the common sight of people with three or four remaining teeth. She didn't owe anyone anything in this place. Xerxes and Shibuya stood watching the trailers, whose parts were moving in the wind. Shibuya's ears twitched, and she took tiny steps here and there. She was a Greyhound mix and easily intimidated. Xerxes stared stoically at one trailer whose siding had been mostly stripped.

Helen came once a week. Early on, she had asked for a discount, her farm was dying because of the drought. Jenny agreed to ten dollars, she enjoyed Helen's company. The woman was in her early forties and had kept her youthful figure. She took care of her feet, which were long and narrow, and she didn't have the vacant, suffering stare Jenny saw on so many people in Querosa. "I've taken classes at the college, I'm an academia nut," she said her first time in Jenny's office.

She'd made that joke before, Jenny could tell. It was the lack of money that had cut Helen's university career short. Money, and five kids. But there seemed to be a different story hiding behind her breezily-told explanation. Jenny couldn't see it yet, but she could feel it clearly, just like the pain in her abdomen.

Her youngest child, a boy, slept in the stroller while she took off her socks. She had a low arch. There was intelligence in a good foot. You could see if people thought with their feet or merely regarded them as something to stomp around on. Helen had good feet, a bit shy, but ready to come out and play. But what intrigued Jenny the most, was that Helen had six toes on each foot. She'd barely noticed the first time.

"I wanted to get them removed," Helen explained. "Ever since I was a little girl. People called me freak, and while my parents didn't care and wouldn't have spent money on the surgery anyway, I was saving dimes and quarters for that surgery. I never went barefoot and always wore clunky shoes to hide my condition. I knew I would get those toes removed once I turned sixteen, and then I had my then-boyfriend drive me to Lubbock to the doctor, and he looked at my toes and asked why I wanted to remove them. Just like that. He asked, 'Who said five toes were any better than six?' And suddenly I didn't want to get rid of my sixth toes anymore. I suddenly understood that I had been worrying about the wrong thing, and the next day I gave all that money I had saved to the church, except for fifty bucks. And with those fifty bucks I bought a pair of nice sandals."

Jenny nodded, wrapping her hands around Helen's foot. Despite the six toes, it wasn't a kinky foot, though there was the faint smell of her Puritan forefathers about it.

Helen also had three teenage boys, nineteen, seventeen and sixteen, and a fourteen-year-old girl. The baby had not been planned. "One of our wells has gone dry already," she said. "If this drought continues, we might as well drown ourselves while there's still water enough in the others."

She couldn't pay the full price, but after the first month of coming to see Jenny, she brought something wrapped in old Christmas paper. "It's nothing," she said. But when Jenny unwrapped the gift, it was a small cross-stitch sampler in a frame.

"You made this yourself," Jenny said.

"My god, you're a psychic." Helen laughed, exposing a slight overbite, and her strong, yellow, teeth.

The sampler was of a small house on fire, and instead of the usual blessings, it said, "It's getting hot in here." Jenny laughed, and Helen joined in. She seemed very pleased with Jenny's reaction, flattered. Her cheeks turned red.

Jenny took off one of the paintings she'd brought from LA and hung Helen's house in that spot. "You're an artist," she said.

"If I could sell them, I'd be one."

"Have you tried?"

Helen shook her head. "Here? In Querosa?"

They both laughed.

"What will happen to our farm? Will it rain?" Helen asked after putting her foot in Jenny's lap.

Jenny's visions were often black and white, blurry, full of atmosphere and feelings, but with little concrete information. She had learned to translate the moods, in the way near-deaf people translated sounds and lip movement into language. Now she concentrated on the farm, on Helen's warm feet, the smell of home-cooked food that clung to her clothes.

"I don't think you'll be moving any time soon," Jenny said cautiously. Yet what she saw wasn't pretty. Shadows moved into her field of vision, and she yelped with sudden pain.

"That bad?" Helen asked.

"No," Jenny tried to assure her. "It's me. I should have myself checked out."

"What's wrong?"

Jenny shook her head. Talking about her lower abdomen seemed unprofessional. Yet even though she had opened her eyes, the pictures hadn't left her mind. Somebody seemed to be spilling dark ink over them. Blocked TV channels in hotel rooms produced similar pictures. A shoulder, a bare breast would fall into focus and then out again. You could recognize only a certain flow, but everything turned liquid. Something was moving underneath the darkness, but you only saw ripples, nothing stayed long enough to be fully recognized.

"I don't think you'll lose your farm, but it'll be tough. I don't see any rain?"

"Can you produce it?"

Jenny wanted to laugh but she suddenly understood that this was the one question Helen had meant to ask all along. Her face was serious, harsh even. Her curvy lips had turned into one thick straight line.

She didn't tell Carl about Yucca Lows. When he returned from his trip, his face and neck and arms burnt, she was disappointed and relieved. In the evening they walked through the lettered streets despite a steady wind that made them spit out dust and grit. The small houses white, beige, or tan, the yards filled with leftovers of leftovers. Cars that would never run again and not provide the right parts. Toys that had been broken and forgotten. Trash made to look like antique ornaments. Whole yards were filled with painstakingly arranged debris.

In front of a tan house with a broken door, a Shepherd mix was chained to the bumper of a Chevy Celebrity missing its wheels. He jumped at them, tearing himself violently off the ground. It was still in the high nineties and the front yard didn't provide any shaded spots. The dog's hips seemed misshapen. Carl stopped, his eyes very clear and yet without readable expression. He stood and watched the dog tear at his chain.

After a few minutes, a man in a John Deere T-shirt appeared in the doorway and watched them watching his dog. The Shepherd's body seemed to curl up in a difficult dance routine, his body writhed. The man closed the screen behind him. "You ain't Mexican," he said.

Carl didn't answer. His demeanor didn't change.

"That dog knows Mexicans."

"How much for the dog?" asked Carl.

"He'll bark. He'll go nuts. Nothing like what he did just now."

"How much?"

The man stepped down, watched the skies for a moment, then spit on the ground. "You got a cigarette?"

Carl shook his head.

"My daddy, he put him in a potato sack. Beat him up good. Used my granddaddy's cane. The first thing that dog saw when Daddy opened the bag was a Mexican, daddy made sure of that. That dog remembers it real well, too. Had him for two years now."

"How much?"

Jenny didn't want a third dog. Jenny didn't want a Mexican-hating Shepherd. She already hated that panting and miserable creature. And yet she kept quiet. She was hurting when she looked at Carl's face. No stone could have been smoother than his face in that moment. And she grabbed her wallet and handed Carl all she had and it was enough to get the dog and a dirty black leash. The dog didn't make a sound when Carl pulled him away from his home. Stunned, he let himself be dragged off.

The first male customer who returned for a second session was a young man driving an 80s Firebird he had painted in black primer. It struck her that he didn't seem proud or in love with the car the way another eighteen or nineteen-year-old would have. When he sat down across from her and she saw his jeans were True Religion and his boots the 300-dollar kind she had her answer. He might have liked the car, but had bought it because he knew what others liked and envied. He could buy himself another one.

He looked around Jenny's office with curious eyes, large and quick like a bird's, then said in a voice that was part squeak, part gravel, "You're not going to tell me that I'll die tomorrow?"

She didn't answer him. She was used to the nervous crackle of people's insecurities. Most customers didn't acknowledge what they wanted to know the first time around. The awkwardness they felt buried their true question and instead they asked about dates, family, winning the lottery.

And that's what he asked the first time – if a certain girl was in love with him, if they had a future.

They did not.

Would he be successful?

"You have to rephrase that," she answered.

"How?"

"Successful is too relative."

"Will I make a ton of money?"

She smiled. "It will be difficult."

"Because I have spidery toes and my big toe is twice the size it should be?"

"Because you have decisions to make. If you choose safety, you'll be rich. If not, you risk having to struggle."

"Sounds like 'follow your dream' advice."

"I'm not advising," she said quickly. Too quickly. He caught her haste, she could see it.

"So who am I?" he said.

"I'm not a phone book."

"You can't see my name and address?" This wasn't the first time she was challenged to divulge random information. The old joke about the man ringing the psychic's doorbell and leaving after hearing the question "Who is it?" through the door still worked.

"You should know? Shouldn't you? If you can see the future, the truth?"

"This is not a circus trick. I'm not a mentalist." She looked for the power to smile.

"For twenty bucks I don't even get a name?" He was insisting now, his squeaky voice, stuck in an adult vocal change, grew louder. He felt he had the upper hand. People who were smart but had no vision behaved that way. She could see his limitations like a graph or chart painted on his body. She suddenly relaxed, her shoulders lowered themselves.

"What are you afraid of?" she asked. "That you'll disappoint your dad?"

His face tightened. At least he was smart enough to show fear. His smirk didn't move one bit, he kept it up until after he'd taken the twenty from his wallet and paid her. The procedure looked painful.

The next time he came, his demeanor was different. You come a second time, your taunts don't fly anymore. A second visit meant you admitted Jenny's value to you. Unless the visitor pulled a gun because he felt betrayed. Carl had given her a small, illegal canister of tear gas. She hadn't used it yet.

She knew better than to say anything about their last encounter and he sat quietly across from her, not taking off his boots. It was a slow day, the light thick and sugary, too hot to step on the pavement in bare feet. She'd watched two girls try through her window.

"He might do something rash," he said without further introduction. "They might come at night, put me on a plane to Arizona or Nevada."

She wasn't interested. She didn't take the bait. Instead she intended to listen and be uplifting and full of empathy. And yet this afternoon, after the young man's opening lines, she felt deflated, her empathy was on its way out. She recognized that sign, and felt herself stiffening. It was like taking off her glasses, she couldn't see anything but blurred contours. A mild depression, an hour in the dentist's waiting room. Numbness settled in.

She still listened yet the words did not connect anymore.

Instead she watched his hair that hadn't been washed in a while, his shell necklace. She didn't want anything from this place. His jeans, long, and dirty at the bottom, were a code she knew. This boy was what filtered through television shows and chain stores, hip reincarnated as a Dillard's sale. She had no hope.

And she couldn't see him anymore. No, the only thing she saw was him, nothing else, no access to his aura. He was just a young man in expensive knock-offs. How could anyone exist? Why did they live?

"And?" he asked. He must have asked before, she could feel a faint echo of that question. And she was holding on to something she'd recognized about him earlier, a minor and major thing, a detail she couldn't see anymore but knew to be there.

"Why don't you just tell him you're gay?"

Laughter made his skin ripple. She thought of the porn Carl watched, movies that showed up in the history of his computer. Not that she searched for them, but when she'd typed in 'an' for animal shelter in the search bar, it had given her analhub.com. The boy's flesh shook. He still hadn't given her his name.

"He'd kill me."

FOUR

Semjâzâ taught enchantments, and root-cuttings, 'Armârôs the resolving of enchantments, Barâqîjâl astrology, Kôkabêl the constellations, Êzêqêêl the knowledge of the clouds, Araqiêl the signs of the earth, Shamsiêl the signs of the sun, and Sariêl the course of the moon. And as men perished, they cried, and their cry went up to heaven...

THE DROUGHT TURNED THEIR LAWN INTO A BEACH, deep, yellow sand, fine and soft. Its surface was rippling, undulating, seven snakes wide. She had to block out future projects and how did you live in a present that hurt like walking across a field of goatheads? Had the saints lived in the moment? Their feet boiled in oil, their flesh barbecued, their heads sawed off? Or had they fled to some inner sanctum, their pseudo-nirvana, a vision of the afterlife? Jenny made a mental note to meditate—she didn't want to steal away to the afterlife.

The mood in town darkened, flies hovered in front of the sun, their noise in the bushes in front of their house saved her. They were bushes she had only ever seen in cemeteries. Campus turned into dunes, trees cracked open, the sky was dust. Every gust of wind rendered her blind.

Abbadona, Adramelec, Agares, Amezyarak, Amy, Anmael, Arakiel, Araziel, Ariel, Arioch, Armaros, Armen, Artaqifa, Asbeel, Asmoday, Asmodeus Astaroth, Astoreth, Atarculph, Auza, Azaradel, Azazel, Azza, Azzael, Balam, Baraqel, Barbatos, Barbiel, Batarjal, Beelzebub, Beliar, Busasejal, Byleth, Balberith, Caim, Carnivean, Carreau, Dagon, Danjal, Ezekeel, Flauros, Gaap, Gadreel, Gressil, Hakael, Hananel, Harut, Iblis, Ielahih, Invart, Jeqon, Jetrel, Kasdeja, Lauiah, Leviathan, Lucifer, Mammon, Marchosias, Marut, Mephistopheles, Meresin, Moloch, Mulciber, Murmur, Nelchael, Nilaihah, Oeillet, Olivier, Ouzza, Paimon, Penemue, Procell, Pursan, Raum, Rimmon, Rosier, Rumael, Sammael, Samsaweel, Saraknyal, Sariel, Satan, Sealiah, Semyaza, Senciner, Shamshiel, Simapesiel, Sonneillon, Tabaet, Thammuz, Tumael, Turael, Turel, Urakbarameel, Usiel, Verrier, Verrine, Vual, Yomyael, Zavebe.

The book of angels said nothing about Querosa, and yet, with sixty churches in town, Jenny took it for a sign.

They named their dog Diesel. The shepherd part was very visible, the other was Bloodhound. He peed on the sofa the first time he entered the living room, after that, never did it again.

He was a mouth-breather, loud and obnoxious, and despite his obvious sweetness—he followed Carl around the house and sat down where Carl sat, accepted Xerxes as his boss and played tirelessly with Shibuya—Jenny couldn't love him. He grated on her, he was a big bumbler, not unlike Carl, but without any grace. He just thought everybody should love him, and she couldn't. Far from it, whenever he approached Shibuya, she had the urge to kick him and drive him off. She didn't like his large, brutish paws, his swaying gait, his immense appetite for food. Diesel ate twice as much as the others and still couldn't gain a pound. When Jenny looked at him, she saw his previous owner's hatred, seemed to smell the inside of that small house with the broken door.

Carl scolded her when he finally noticed. He took Diesel on walks, put him in his truck whenever he went to a dig. He had upset the balance in the house, Jenny felt. It sounded silly to her own ears.

"From LA?" their dinner host said, his lips curling. "LA," he repeated, possibly looking for the worst cliché he could put on their plates. This contempt she knew, everyone outside of LA had it. LA, the garish faux-blonde in tasteless clothing, with a tucked tummy, filled breasts, insisting she's a star. Jenny was no longer interested in her Chardonnay. California, less than Napa.

The food was German, Sauerbraten, and excellent. Bernie was a history teacher. His wife Sybil looked like she might make a good wife for Carl. That thought presented itself in Jenny's head like a billboard. Sybil was a tall brunette, athletic. Bernie was expansive and balding, he didn't fit. Jenny couldn't remember why they had been invited.

"Do you miss it?" Sybil asked.

Jenny looked at her clean face and its large, clean features, slowly returning to the conversation. Did she? She shook her head. "Not much."

"All the traffic," Bernie said as if he knew.

"The smog sometimes," Jenny said. "The colors. Definitely the colors. The new cars. All shiny, glitzy dreams. I miss the cars."

Sybil smiled. "Smoked salmon. And Trader Joe's. My cousin lives in the Valley. When I was in college, I visited her often. I miss the food. Last week I went to a conference in Boston and outside the convention center was this grocery store, Shaw's, and I went in to get some wine and it was just a regular, big grocery store, and my eyes were suddenly so full. All that cheese."

Carl wasn't listening. Big Carl, his eyes glazed since 'convention center.' Off he went into his own world, without malice or guilt, he could tune out everyone's remarks.

"Carl," the host said. "Let me show you my baby." Then he smirked at Jenny and his wife. "Man stuff."

The wives were left behind, smiling, and as soon as their husbands had left the room, their smiles soured. "What do you do?" Sybil asked.

"I'm a psychic," Jenny sad.

"A sidekick?"

"I read futures," Jenny continued, relieved that this was still news.

"I'm a department secretary," Sybil said without missing a beat. "The wives are all department secretaries. The husbands never are."

"What is Bernie showing to Carl?"

"His Challenger. It'll take them a while. He'll pop the hood and start it up. The sound. He's all about the sound. Come." She stood up and led Jenny down a hallway. "This is his man cave." The light came on and exposed swords hanging on the walls. An old rifle was mounted above the closet. "World War II," Sybil explained. "His granddad collected."

"What is this?" asked Jenny, pointing to some hideously impressive sword.

"Conan. A movie prop. It was really used during filming."

"It looks smaller than I would have imagined."

"And those are 19th century cavalry sabers."

"Small too."

"Yes, they are. But don't mention it to Bernie. He'll pout for the rest of the evening."

"What do you know about plans for a new car plant in Querosa?"

Sybil looked at her with a blank face, only her lips were parted a little. Then she switched off the light in Bernie's man cave, and together the women walked back to the dining room. "That's just a rumor," Sybil said, "but it refuses to die. I heard that the local bank is buying properties outside of town. A developer, Mitchell or Mitchum, supposedly is in on the deal. Or he's doing his own thing. But I first heard about this plan five years ago, when we moved to Querosa. And we still don't have a car plant in town. Yet the real estate prices have risen. In this hellhole, houses should be dirt cheap, but we pay as much as in Santa Fé."

"I was told that rich Californians are visiting the town."

Sybil took a new bottle of wine from the fridge and opened it. "To rich Californians," she said with a crooked smile and filled the glasses to the top.

"To rich Californians. Do you have a woman cave?" Jenny asked. They could hear the engine of the Challenger bellowing, then shrieking.

"I call that the master bathroom. Bernie is not allowed. Can't stand his hair covering everything. He's only allowed to use the guest bathroom."

Later at home, they showered together, and Carl propped her against the wall. "Did you have a good time?" he asked after he'd found a comfortable standing position and inserted himself.

"Was the car that good?" she asked. She soaped her breasts, feeding him images from his computer, his eyes were wide.

"Pretty good. 1971. No rust. But he doesn't have the Hemi. The engine looks smaller than what you'd think."

"How did you like Sybil?"

"Pretty. But no tits, flat ass."

"Hmm," Jenny said, again amazed at her husband's taste. Sybil was a stunner, and he hadn't noticed. Or did he pretend? Did he work off his appetite for Sybil right now? "And her stomach?"

"If I wanted to sleep with an ant, she'd be perfect."

She soaped more, he thrust harder, chafing her. And she didn't stop him, she could feel his heart beat out of his chest and enjoyed his lust for her more than his churning body. She felt safe, not satisfied. She knew how to handle that other thing herself. Her legs were wobbly.

She first saw him one morning scaling the cinderblock wall and leaving their yard. The dogs made no noise, but two followed the apparition with mild curiosity, their noses dulled from cow dung and ethanol. Not even Diesel got up to bark. When she looked toward the chain link gate, a small body flew by and the only thing she could make out was a faded Superman shirt.

He was skinny, that much was immediately

apparent, even though she only saw half of him the next time, an early morning ten days later, when nausea and itching had awakened her and she let out the dogs early. It was 4:30 and the sky only just turning lighter and the yard light came on and he peered out from the doghouse Carl had built to give Shibuya a hiding place when Diesel got too rambunctious. She opened the screen door and he took off, just like the first time. He wore stained shorts and the same Superman shirt, he couldn't be much older than six or seven.

FIVE

There is one wise and greatly to be feared, the Lord sitting upon his throne.

He created her, and saw her, and numbered her, and poured her out upon all his works.

She is with all flesh according to his gift, and he hath given her to them that love him.

The fear of the Lord is honour, and glory, and gladness, and a crown of rejoicing.

The fear of the Lord maketh a merry heart, and giveth joy, and gladness, and a long life.

Whoso feareth the Lord, it shall go well with him at the last, and he shall find favour in the day of his death. To fear the Lord is the beginning of wisdom: and it was created with the faithful in the womb. She hath built an everlasting foundation with men, and she shall continue with their seed. To fear the Lord is fulness of wisdom, and filleth men with her fruits. She filleth all their house with things desirable, and the garners with her increase.

HELEN'S FARM WAS NORTHWEST OF TOWN, past a collection of trailers with dogs that had never known a leash. They rushed at the car, blocked her way, and when she slowed down, jumped up at her window. They looked at Jenny full of hunger and hatred.

She saw the cloud, which she had taken for a dust devil, long before she recognized the red pick-up. It came right at her, the windshield tinted against the sun. Only when she glanced at the half-open driver's window did she see J.D. Hartt's face, partially covered by a large, white cowboy hat. The truck wasn't anything special. Big, relatively new, but just a regular Ford. Not a Lincoln or Cadillac. In her rearview mirror she saw the NObamacare sticker on his bumper. He gave them away for free at all of his bank's branches.

The farmhouse was a manufactured home, spruced up with stucco to appear adobe. A small trailer stood in back. One half seemed to be intact, the other had been torn apart, ransacked, and its parts turned into two chicken coops.

"You're the white witch."

He didn't seem friendly or unfriendly. He was a big man, almost as tall as Carl, but flabby, with a dirty blue t-shirt, jeans, boots and a white cowboy hat. His eyes nearly disappeared in the folds of his flesh. He stood in the door and more than anything looked like a gigantic baby. An apprehensive baby. Suspicion kept his face expressionless.

"I'm Jenny," she said and forced a grin onto her face. "Helen is expecting me. Did Hartt pay you a visit?"

"You alone?" He stepped outside, closing the door behind him. He stared at her car, looked left and right. He took his time, didn't look her way.

"Is Helen here?" The presence of the old Geo Metro seemed to say so. "Does he want to buy your farm?"

"You're not from here, are you?" Dan said.

"You have a nice farm," she said.

"If you come back in two weeks, you can have it for twenty bucks. We go to church every Sunday. Can't say I enjoy it, but I haven't missed a Sunday in twelve years."

"But you wouldn't mind if I fixed your well for you." Jenny opened her purse and retrieved her car keys. She made sure Dan saw it too. "Well, I got to go." She walked back to her Subaru and when she had her hand on the door handle, he said, "Yeah, she's here."

Dan turned, opened the house door and disappeared inside. The screen slapped shut, but the other was a gaping black rectangle. Noises from a television show reached her, laughter and applause.

"He's not mean," Helen told her when she'd extracted a pitcher from the refrigerator and put chocolate chip cookies on the kitchen table. "He's worried. He isn't very *suave*." She grinned, but again, Jenny couldn't see beyond what Helen was showing her. She seemed genuinely sorry for her husband's behavior, and yet something didn't seem to fit. "Wanna have some iced coffee?"

They sat down, and for the first minute, they remained silent. Then Helen said, "It's not much. And it's not yet ours. If the drought continues we'll have to sell."

"Who would want it? Was Hartt here to make you an offer?"

"The second time already."

"Are you trying to get more money?"

Helen grinned again. "This time he offered half. He knows that soon he can have it for free. There's enough interest, but we're running out of time to negotiate. Word is the base is looking to expand. That, and Sam's Club might build a distribution center here. But there's more to it."

Jenny waited for her to continue, but Helen only smiled. "And?"

"Here's what I've heard. Don't know if it's true. They're gonna build a car manufacturing plant here. The state is desperate, and Texas is next door, where they sell all their trucks. Tax incentives, lax eco standards, whatever they want. If we can hold on to this land long enough we might be rich one day." She laughed loud and harsh. "Then I'm gonna buy myself a Bentley. Maybe a used one."

Jenny nodded, didn't tell Helen that she'd already heard the story. In Los Angeles, people had been waiting for more than thirty years for a subway line connecting downtown with Santa Monica. And still nothing had happened. Nobody had become rich. Every five or ten years new rumors were dragged through the presses and then immediately mothballed.

The women could hear a roaring exhaust, and moments later an old truck pulled into the yard. The doors opened and three boys got out. They all wore white cowboy hats, jeans, and spurs.

A few seconds later they stood in the kitchen, silent, staring at Jenny as though she were holding a gun to their mother's head. "That's her, isn't it?" the tallest and heaviest of them said. He had the face of his mother and the heavy-set body of his father. "Was Hartt here? We saw his truck."

Helen nodded. "That's my friend Jenny." She gestured toward her sons. "Tim, Jared, Gabe."

Gabe was the oldest, but it was Jared, the middle one, who was the most striking. He'd taken off his hat, and his hair reached over his ears. It was exquisitely blond, and Jenny imagined that people felt the urge to touch it, it shone so invitingly. A pet rabbit couldn't have been any softer. Tim, the youngest was a smaller version of his father, his eyes tiny and full of malice. He had the largest feet of the three.

"Is she gonna do it?" Gabe asked.

"Gabe!" Helen's voice was sharp, and she seemed to grow on her chair, as though she might spread her wings and breathe fire.

"That's why she's here, isn't it."

"That's right," Jenny said, before Helen found the time to answer. "That's why I'm here. But I'm a psychic. I see things, I don't move or alter them."

"So why you're here?" Tim asked, then opened the refrigerator and pulled out a Coke.

"Enough." In the fraction of a second, Helen stood in front of Tim, grabbed the Coke and slapped his face. "Next time you ask."

Tim glowered, then left. He didn't look back at Jenny. Only Jared took his time, lingered a second longer. He was all his mother and yet did not appear feminine. He winked at Jenny, then slowly followed his brothers.

"Too much testosterone, way, way too much. And too silly to have girlfriends and burn it off."

"They work with Dan?"

"We need every one of them. And they know it. They're good boys, but they know we're drowning."

Jenny nodded.

"We borrowed a rig from someone who owed us a favor. The boys are looking for the right spot. If all goes well, they'll start drilling in a few days."

Jenny drank her coffee, which was weak and only tasted of cream and sugar, the way you bought it at McClellan's and at Daybreak Donuts. Helen didn't touch the cookies.

After ten minutes Dan entered the kitchen. His face still didn't move, his eyes didn't meet hers. He stood as though over an open grave. His humility frightened Jenny.

"Yes, I'm ready now," she said.

Dan drove, and next to him sat Jared and Gabe. Jenny and Helen sat sideways in back. The truck groaned and behind them all Jenny could see was dust. She knew what Helen expected from her, realized she had known and shouldn't have come. The back of her shirt clung to her skin. The AC was working, but she barely registered it. She fingered her abdomen, which was full of small, unknown pains. She tried to breathe into that region but to no avail. The pain only increased.

After fifteen minutes Dan stopped next to an old work truck carrying a rig. He got out without a word, and his boys followed. Jared held Jenny's door open. "Ma'am."

The spot didn't look special or promising to her, it appeared like any other spot in the desert. "Show me the exact location," she ordered Jared.

The boy marched some thirty yards to his left, then turned to smile at her. "Here."

"Gentleman farmer." Carl drove them along a narrow, tree-lined road up to Hartt's estate. She hated the word *estate*, preferred *compound*, despite its militaristic connotation. There was a bocce court in front of a terrace, the buildings were low and sand-colored, old adobe structures with barns and two silos to the right. But they had taken a wrong turn, the reception was in a different building off to the left, a woman dressed like a maid told them.

She hadn't told Carl of her afternoon at Helen's ranch, nor did she mention the pain in her abdomen. The well hadn't caused it, she was certain. Supernatural powers had nothing to do with it.

Dan and Helen had been disappointed with her. She hadn't thrown herself to the ground, foamed at the mouth, or spouted unintelligible words. Nothing had moved within her. "Not today," she had put Helen off. "Soon. Soon. I'll come back."

The parking lot was filled with BMWs and Mercedes they had never seen in town. A pool seemed to hover in front of the old, colonial building, its bottom an old-fashioned blue. A picture taken many years ago. Lights hung in the trees, a piano played somewhere inside.

"I didn't know something like this existed in Querosa." Her eyes were full of green, she'd never seen so many trees out here. Guests swarmed the garden and the terrace, though nobody seemed to pay attention to the pool. She took off her sandals, sat down on the red tile before Carl could grab her arm and hold her back. The water was cool, and she noticed a light film on its surface, leaves too. The pool wasn't meant for swimming, she failed to smell chlorine.

The stares drove her up, barely polite stares from guests in suits and women in impossible, flower-patterned dresses, as though Jenny had drunk baptismal water.

She followed Carl inside, followed the sound of the piano, followed her husband into another era. The lights from the garden dimmed and the ballroom was tinged sepia. The chandeliers shone brightly, and yet there didn't seem to be any light in this room. Pop had not been invented in its time.

Waiters offered small bites on silver platters. Jenny noticed that only half the people seemed to live in town, only the obese, badly dressed ones. The others she found remarkably handsome and dressed accordingly. For the first time since moving to Querosa she felt underdressed in a striped cotton dress. But where was J.D.? Jenny gyrated as politely as Carl's presence required, she didn't want to embarrass him or turn his thoughts into hungry rats.

A few faces from university functions lit up and fell dark again. Carl towered a head over the crowd, his own lighthouse.

J.D. wore a white jacket, the relative darkness of the ballroom allowed him to look clean, clad in near shadows. Carl, big Carl, shrank to a boy in his presence. J.D. dominated, his face so much closer to hers, his face full of lines the missing light accentuated. Carl was awash in illuminated planes, so young and silly he looked. He looked better, younger, and much, much stronger than J.D., and still he couldn't touch him.

"What does J.D. stand for?' Jenny asked.

"You don't have anything to drink," he answered. He wasn't handsome, his face was loosening, his hair turning gray, and she forgot about her husband towering over her, the enthusiastic puppy. She looked greedily at J.D.'s hands, the slight gut he was pushing and the hundred-dollar shirt could not conceal. He smelled of wood and Cabernet and the wine glass was a daisy he'd plucked for her and she took it and said, "I'll have what you're having."

Then he was off to greet new guests and Carl returned from the bar with a Stella and looked unhappy. "You were rude," he said and she nodded up at his face and smiled and said, "Yes, yes, I was."

Bernie and Sybil appeared, Bernie's eyes already glazed, Sybil's curious. "Was that Hartt?" she said. "I'd imagined him to look like a cowboy. Or Wyatt Earp. Handlebar mustache." Carl and Bernie clinked bottles, drank. Sybil scratched a rash below her chin. Bernie's eyes were mercury, she couldn't stand watching them. They appeared diseased, bloated, ready to burst. The face harboring them was red and whoever had made it, had not been fond of it and neglected to finish its surfaces. She wanted to cross out that thought, it lacked generosity, but J.D.'s presence made her restless. She was sweaty from the effort not to hurry after their host.

To the ladies' room she escaped, mingled with unknown women in the antechamber, an eclectic mix of antique knick-knacks and photographs making it appear to have survived centuries, though she was sure that no such history existed. When it was her turn, she shrank from her reflection, the dark spots on her dress, her dry neck, her sunburned shoulders. She looked like Carl's territory again, good enough for Carl, Carl-ish, Carl's toy. A woman without need for style and no sense for it either.

Big cities assured you that you never ran into your clients if you preferred not to, but here were two faces and two pairs of feet she recognized. She lowered her gaze, hurried away.

She stopped at the bar, ready to take on Carl and Sybil with a new glass of wine, then slipped out into the garden. There'd be an excuse, it would come to her.

She retreated to the pool, ashamed suddenly, and disappointed, dipping her feet, those two red orphans, into the filmy waters.

"I wouldn't do that," a voice behind her said and she recognized it even though she'd never been good at recognizing actors in animated movies and couldn't have identified Carl's voice on the phone, fifteen years back, in the age of landlines.

"They keep sharks?" she asked.

"Bad memories."

"Of naked feet?"

He crouched beside her, came much closer than he'd ever been in her office.

"How do you like it here? Are you with your parents? Do you know J.D.'s children?"

He smiled with squinting eyes, unsure, maybe, if she was trying to humor him. "I'm Garrett." He wore canvas sneakers tonight, the eternal expression of aspiring hipness. "You really shouldn't do this."

She fished her feet out of the pool and put them in front of Garrett. "Why not?"

"Aaron drowned here."

Her insight was immediate, took no time at all, but she hadn't seen it coming. A blanket had been pulled off an architectural model and she saw everything at once: the history of this place and Garrett's position in it.

"How did you make it happen?"

"I pretended I couldn't get any air."

She put a hand to his face, not to console him, maybe just to signal he had no obligation to her. "And since then..."

"Nobody has used the pool."

"Why not just get...?"

"It wouldn't get rid of the memories. It's Aaron's memorial, the place where he's almost present. You can almost hear him swallowing water."

"He was younger."

"By four years." He told her he'd pretended to drown and Aaron had jumped after him. Garrett let himself sink to the bottom and counted, and when he finally came up for air, his brother was already dead. "I did everything I'd seen people do in the movies." He touched her right foot. "I killed his man-son," he said.

They huddled together, music and voices behind them, a curtain in front of the floor to ceiling windows rendering them invisible.

"He's not forgiven you," she said.

"He would have. But he already knew. About me. He always knew."

"You're still here."

That truth sat inside his body, and the image she had of it was that of a metal rod people used to support a bush or tree.

"I came to see you."

"To receive a future?"

"Some place that might have me."

"You can choose one."

"I need more than that."

"A reason?"

"I can't go until…"

"He'll never love you," she said, forgetting all caution. She had seen that line as though it had appeared on the surface of the pool, she just had to voice it. "Not your fault. He's just not that kind of man."

"What kind?"

The question puzzled her and shook her out of whatever state of mind she'd been in. She looked more closely at Garrett and suddenly disliked him, as though she'd turned into his father. "I shouldn't," she said.

"Get in the water?" J.D. stood behind them, towering, even though Garrett was taller than his dad when he got up and straightened his limbs. The boy turned away and disappeared, his father a gale force, he a mere leaf. Yet whatever storm Garrett had felt, it died down once he left the terrace.

"Where's your husband?" He helped her up, his hand dry, his finger nails neatly filed.

She shrugged happily. "God knows."

He took her arm and led her out into the garden. They couldn't see Querosa, only the glow of the city. "You have a white peacock?" she asked. "I've heard stories."

"He's hiding," J.D. said lightly, unconcerned. "Few people have seen him."

She took his glass, her own she'd abandoned at the pool. "People are afraid of you," she said.

He shrugged, nothing in his face moved.

"They come to me to be assured that they're still in your good graces. Or they come to find out you still don't like them. Your own son stays in Querosa because you don't love him."

"You must know, you're the psychic," he said. "Which kind are you?"

"The third one," she said, giggling, barely registering his condescending tone. She felt safe here, didn't need to know why. Tomorrow she'd regret her tipsiness, her urge to let other people know what she knew, this vanity, this small-girl classroom behavior, the I-know-the-answer eagerness. She detested it, but now she followed it with giddiness.

In the parking lot she kissed him.

"Which one is that?"

"I'm infatuated with you," she said.

He pushed her against the fender of a black Audi, lifted her dress, her left leg.

"Not that infatuated." She escaped, with a bit of scotch still in his glass. "You'll need to earn me, Mr. Hartt." Then she took off, ran back to his house, back to Carl, back to everything she knew and her place in this town and world.

She was up at 4:00, the dogs happy to see her. This time the pain was excruciating and she vomited, tried not to wake Carl. She took several Aleve, curled up on the couch, Shibuya and Diesel huddling around her. I can't be pregnant, she thought, but just thinking it made it seem almost plausible. I would *know* if I were pregnant. I need to see a doctor.

The clinic in town looked like an extended trailer park, and people with serious conditions were flown by helicopter to Texas. She'd heard all the stories about misdiagnoses, botched prescriptions, failed emergency procedures. "Don't get sick here," people had told her more than once, always with the same crooked smile.

Her doctor was Hispanic, a petite woman with glasses and an easy smile. "My first year here, a lot of the old people wouldn't let me touch them. They barely talked to me."

Jenny sat on the fold-out table, in bra and skirt. "Because you were not from here?"

"Because I'm not white." Caroline Moncayo's feet were stuck in sandals, her toes very short and broad.

"But half the town is Mexican," Jenny said. The pain had subsided, but she could feel its echo. She couldn't sit up straight.

"But one half pretends the other half isn't here. Thing is, I'm from Santa Fé, if you ask my dad, he's white."

"But things must have changed quite a bit,"

Jenny said. The stethoscope moved over her abdomen.

"Not as long as the old guard owns the town. We couldn't even get a space for Democratic headquarters during the last election. Nobody would lease their buildings, even though most of them were empty."

"J.D. Hartt?" Jenny asked.

Dr. Moncayo walked over to her desk, retrieved her laptop and started to type. Then she looked up at Jenny. It wasn't clear if she was smiling or silently chiding her patient. "Him too."

The scan had to be sent to a Texas hospital, and Jenny was waiting on a gurney, behind green curtains. A nurse checked on her from time to time. She called Carl and only got his voice mail. She read her e-mails, and they were all advertising. She tried to read the LA Times on her phone, but she had forgotten her glasses, and after ten minutes she felt a headache form behind her eyes.

S I X

Thou wast perfect in thy ways from the day that thou wast created, till iniquity was found in thee. By the multitude of thy merchandise they have filled the midst of thee with violence, and thou hast sinned: therefore I will cast thee as profane out of the mountain of God: and I will destroy thee, O covering cherub, from the midst of the stones of fire. Thine heart was lifted up because of thy beauty, thou hast corrupted thy wisdom by reason of thy brightness: I will cast thee to the ground, I will lay thee before kings, that they may behold thee. Thou hast defiled thy sanctuaries by the multitude of thine iniquities, by the iniquity of thy traffick; therefore will I bring forth a fire from the midst of thee, it shall devour thee, and I will bring thee to ashes upon the earth in the sight of all them that behold thee. All they that know thee among the people shall be astonished at thee: thou shalt be a terror, and never shalt thou be any more.

HE TOOK THE CHICKEN, THE HAM. The bread he seemed to dislike. He didn't look cute when he ate, not like her dogs. His breath was as foul as theirs.

He still wore his Superman shirt, his dirty sneakers. She kept boxes of lunchmeat for the dogs, treats to lure them inside, to lure them into the garage and into their crate. They couldn't resist, she loved them for that weakness. Dog boy couldn't resist either. He had small teeth, brown they were, his arms were full of scabs. He didn't seem to like or trust her, there was no smile. But she was dependable.

When she sat down in the backyard, the sun was still low enough to keep the heat bearable. He sat down in front of her, squatted like Xerxes or Shibuya, then snapped up the next slice of ham. A truck came driving down the back alley and sent him to the corner of the yard and he half-jumped, half-climbed up on top of the cinderblock wall and was gone. The cupcake she'd brought he'd left untouched. Her coffee too.

After two more weeks she could count on his arm sticking out from the opening of the dog house, or a dirty foot. The dogs accepted him, for what she had no idea. They sniffed him the way they sniffed each other, always curious to detect new scents and read the history of his exploits outside the yard.

He waited his turn. In the mornings, first Xerxes, the oldest, was fed. Then Shibuya, their princess, received her meal, stretched, yawned, waited to be petted, and slowly started on the kibble. Diesel was last, and he'd learned not to touch the others' food the hard way. He would never look normal, his hip had been broken and healed incorrectly, yet he had this sunny, silly demeanor, and he was eager to run for miles with Carl. When Carl sped up, Diesel tucked in his weak leg and kept up on three. He was ferocious, single-minded, and loyal. He was Carl with bad hips and a limp. He was a beautiful dog.

Dog boy did not receive dry food; soon she'd learned what he preferred. Apricots and mangoes were his favorite. Meats. He took little else, hated candy. And only drank water. No coffee, soda, or juice. He drank from the dogs' bowls.

"What's your name?" she asked one day.

He stared at her, cocked his head, even his ears twitched.

"Do you have a name?" She put a bowl of mango slices in front of him. She pointed at the dogs, told him their names.

"Haag," he said.

"Haag," she repeated. He growled at her.

The week a fire destroyed a ranch on the way to Caldwell, he started coming earlier at night, before she fed Xerxes one last time. The dog's stomach couldn't go a whole night without food. She saw dog boy shit in one corner of the yard, then cover his feces with loose dirt.

The drought had made the trees on campus die by then. Trees died all around Querosa, the police patrolled the streets to catch those watering their gardens. It wasn't about the lawns anymore, everybody had given up on the lawns.

Neighbors ratted each other out to the cops. If your bushes had survived, they'd stand by the fence, watching your house after sunset. Just making sure. Dust colored the sky, every gust of wind drove sand into Jenny's eyes. Cattle died or, if the farmers were lucky enough, were sold off half-starved. Patches of road melted, the horizon at dusk shimmered in myriad tones of orange, all of them dirty.

An old couple died when their swamp cooler broke. They'd lived in town for eighty-two years. Jenny left the house to run at four in the morning and on the day Mr. and Mrs. Stimworth were found dead in their home on Avenue G, she saw that people had moved into the abandoned trailers south of town. She saw the cars first. Malibus and Impalas, but mostly trucks, too many of them, too many for the cramped spaces that might still be inhabitable in Yucca Lows. Arizona license plates, Louisiana, Texas. None of them from New Mexico. There were no dogs. But she found two dead by the road. Those had harassed her and Shibuya on every run, no matter the hour. They were lying two feet apart from each other, red spots spread over them like polka dots. She counted nineteen cars and trucks for three trailers.

After eight days, during which she hadn't heard from Helen, Jenny drove to the farm a second time. Taking the risk didn't make sense, perhaps it was sheer vanity. Every time she asked herself why she was driving down this dusty road, her thoughts got stuck. She couldn't answer the question, yet she didn't turn around.

The family sat at the dinner table, and nobody offered her a seat. Nobody, not even Helen, got up.

"Have you found water?"

Jared met her eyes and shook his head.

"I'm ready," Jenny said.

It was Dan who left the table and grabbed his hat. He was Jenny's enemy, but he wouldn't forego this opportunity. "Let's go," he said, and his wife and sons put their knives and forks down and followed him outside.

This time, Jenny sat in front, pointed at the setting sun. Dan remained silent and followed her instructions. The pain in her lower abdomen was returning while the pick-up rattled over narrow, sandy paths. Every pothole made Jenny cringe.

She took her time observing Helen's land, pointed a finger every now and then. Perhaps she was merely following her desire to work a miracle, but it didn't matter anymore. Water, she had to find water.

"Stop."

She got out, and Jared followed. After ten minutes she paused, turned to take in her surroundings. She stood next to Helen's pretty son, who didn't belong to his dad. She was absolutely certain, there couldn't be any doubt. He had nothing of Dan's aura.

Then she concentrated on what she might find below. Could she sense the water? Could she tell them that this well would save the farm? She stared at the horizon, three-hundred-sixy degrees of unbroken horizon, and the skies were so large they seemed solid. Red and orange veins ran through them now, and dust made the sun appear twice its size.

Jared stepped away from her, and the others kept their distance. They expected a spectacle, a chant maybe, handwringing and shrill voices. And then she retched, stood stooped in the hot sand, and nothing came. Her abdomen was full of knives, like nothing she'd ever felt. She lowered herself to the ground and gave in to moans that rose up inside her. She had no connection to a higher power, she understood that, and yet she grabbed sand and small stones and flung them about. She owed Helen a spectacle, spectacle was the only way Dan would take her back to the house. Her pain was her insurance that the boys would not put their hands on her.

She understood what she hadn't been able to see before. Dan wasn't the source of this, Dan had nothing to do with it. It was Helen who would order her sons to hold her down. It was Helen, who would happily sacrifice her if that meant water for her farm. Soft, six-toed Helen. These sons were her sons, and four people were enough to kill and bury her. The murder would stay in the family. The land was vast and nobody would know where to start searching for her. She would disappear as though she had drowned in the Pacific.

She was crying when the pain finally subsided, and she smeared her face to let the others know. "Yes," she said, "yes."

SEVEN

And they said unto her, Thou art mad. But she constantly affirmed that it was even so. Then said they, It is his angel.

SHE DROVE TO THE POLICE STATION, waited half an hour until an officer in his fifties led her to his desk. His teeth were small and brown, and maybe that was the reason why he didn't smile. "Scott Streeter," he said as a welcome.

Jenny explained, that she had seen a waif near her house, told Streeter that he ran on all fours. Had anyone reported a six or seven-year-old missing?

Streeter listened her out, sighed. "What would you like to do about it?" he asked. "Does he steal from you? Has he attacked anyone?"

"He must belong to somebody."

The officer nodded. "Sure, sure." He gave her a tight-lipped smile, he seemed to mean well. Yet he didn't pull a piece of paper from his drawer, didn't jot down her address.

"How do you like living in Querosa? Dusty

enough for you?" He spoke with a Texas drawl, every word seemed to have multiple syllables.

"Yes, it's plenty dry here."

"You are the rainmaker?"

"Excuse me?"

"I hope it helps. Can't hurt."

"The boy."

"Yea, yes, the boy. Shame." Streeter didn't move.

She didn't tell them where they could find him. She said a quick goodbye, and Streeter followed her outside and watched her get in her Subaru and drive off. She felt proprietary about Haag. She told herself she had his best interest in mind. How could he survive foster parents, foster homes?

Dr. Moncayo had made the appointment for her, and after she'd postponed it twice for a couple of days, she finally drove to Lubbock. The landscape didn't change during those two hours. If anything, it became more even. There was nothing to see, even the horizon seemed overwhelmed and had abandoned everything to the skies. The clouds took on the color of the fields, and in between hung dust. This was soothing, and yet her eyes, once she had reached the clinic and sat in the dark waiting room, filling out paper work, felt sandpapered. She could hardly see a thing.

The teratoma was as large as a baseball, left of center. It might have teeth, eyes even, the doctor told her. Hair. Feet. Hands. It was as though her womb was trying to assemble a child of its own, without Carl's input. As if her uterus had had enough and didn't want to wait any longer.

"We probably have to perform a supracervial hysterectomy, meaning we won't remove the cervix. If it's bad. But we won't know until we open you up."

The doctor was a man in his sixties, trim, with a gold watch and a fat gold chain around his neck. The shirt stood open and revealed chest hair. Jenny had believed this fashion to be extinct. But she trusted him. She couldn't see his feet, couldn't read the palms of his hands, and yet there was a clean aura about him, Lysol seemed to fill the room.

"And I really need the procedure?"

He looked at her from behind thick glasses, as though she had spoken in Hindi. Then he said, "It's going to get bigger, and we might have to do a total hysterectomy. Spontaneous rupture is rare, but it happens. Perforation into other intra-abdominal organs has been reported. That can include rupture into the bladder, small bowel, rectum, vagina, and even through the abdominal wall."

"How soon?"

"Next week Thursday. Bring your husband. You can't drive afterwards for two weeks. He'll need to tie your shoes too." He smiled.

She shook his hand, then walked to reception desk and paid $400, then was sent to another building, where someone in a suit explained the procedure and gave her several instruction sheets. She paid another $800.

When she arrived in Querosa, she stopped at the McDonald's. The parking lot was empty, the restaurant locked. A poster behind the glass door stated that the location would stay closed for two months. The building would be torn down. Next to the poster was a drawing of the new restaurant.

"Shit, shit, shit, shit." Jenny hit the glass door with her fists. She knew how silly she had to look, but she had fantasized about a real latté for two hours. One of her lifelines had been severed. She cried on the way back to her car.

The weekend they spent in Taos. The landscape rose around them on their drive. Fell and rose again. It was barren and burnt, and yet after months in Querosa, this seemed like the big, wide world. They stopped in Las Vegas, ate green chile stew and tortillas, then headed north again. This was the New Mexico you could see in brochures and advertisements. Mountains, clear creeks, pottery and turquoise jewelry. Tourists and vistas.

They visited the Earth Ships, structures

placed in the dirt and made from recycled materials, bottles, tires, concrete. You could grow vegetables in your living quarters. They were the only structures that made sense in the barren landscape. A touch of Tatooine, a touch of Gaudi's Barcelona. Jagged clouds above like a fleet of destroyers.

They had lunch at a microbrewery and ate German brats. Afterward they hiked down the gorge to sit in the hot springs by the Rio Grande. She expected pain to cut her day short. The knives would shift. Yet the teratoma kept quiet, her child didn't kick or move.

Carl had made the reservations and from the lawn behind their Bed and Breakfast they could overlook the pueblo. Mabel Dodge had lived here with Tony Luhan, had received D.H. Lawrence and Georgia O'Keeffe. This was history, this place connected them to a clear past and countless museum shops and bookstores. This was real, real, real, real.

Carl had brought wine and they got drunk on the view and Cabernet, and in the evening, already drunk and silly, they ate at a small French restaurant housed in an old chapel. They sat where the altar had been and watched well-dressed couples eat their beet and fennel soup and drink bottles of French wine.

"How urban," Carl said.

"Like a real city," Jenny laughed.

"We could be real people."

"Maybe."

He kissed her, smelled of Bordeaux. Candle light flickered on his face, he looked all new and mysterious. Not like a professor at a small university for small Christians. "What was your name again?" she said.

He was quick. "Henry. Henry Breckenridge."

"The Explorer?"

"The same one."

"Tell me about your expedition to the Andes."

"Won't it bore you?"

"Not a chance."

They found a local bar where a band played country and men in white straw hats and spurs two-stepped with women in pink cowboy boots. Henry Breckenridge knew how to lead, she could have jumped onto the tips of his shoes without slowing him down. He was brash, fit in with the local cowboys, he drank their whiskey.

She called him Henry later in their room, muttered his name many times, black beads on a string, and afterward ran her fingers over this beautiful new companion. How much skin, how well-proportioned. And he wasn't hers, she had no obligations. She was a fling, a one night-stand, and he would be off to Australia or Asia the next morning. He was a good time. What wide feet he had.

Eight

*And the beast was taken, and with him the false prophet
that wrought miracles before him, with which he deceived
them that had received the mark of the beast, and them that
worshipped his image. These both were cast alive into a lake
of fire burning with brimstone.*

"You cursed that son of mine." Helen wore boots,
she hadn't come to have Jenny read her fate.
She looked thinner, her jaw was even more pro-
nounced, appeared wider, harder. She looked
younger too, Jenny thought. Jane Birkin of the
Eastern High Plains.

"I didn't."

"They set up the rig, right at the spot where
you did your wild show."

"It wasn't a show."

"Looked real good. They hadn't liked you, but
you sure got their respect. And then the whole
thing collapsed." Helen seemed suddenly exhausted, as though that last sentence had kept
her erect on her way into town and into Jenny's

parlor. Outside the skies were plastered with clouds, but not of the dark, rainy kind. They were brittle, uneven like macaroons and of the same color. Looking at them turned one's mouth dry. Jenny had been on her way home, for her sanity-break. But Helen's truck had stopped her.

"Which one?" Jenny asked.

"You can't even see that?"

There was no need to see anything. "Jared."

"He's in the hospital. Won't walk again. Ever."

"The rig."

"Was perfectly fine. Old yes, but Dan's guy has been using it for years and maintained it well. It's his livelihood."

"And how would I have made it collapse?"

"Is there another explanation?"

"Your sons..."

"You should have seen yourself. Made my blood curdle."

She had never been accused of that much power, and it was a strange taste in her mouth. She had no proof that she wasn't guilty of weakening the metal structure and making the rig collapse, there was no explanation she could give to defend herself. It was as easy as that. She dealt with the supernatural and she had tried to be helpful. Or maybe she had been tempted by vanity. Whatever it was, she couldn't take it back. How many people in town knew that Jared had been hurt? How many people had Helen told that Jenny was responsible?

"That was not the Lord's voice."

"And you would know?"

"That's college talk, real smart. Trying to outdo me."

"You said you were an academia nut."

"And I would hurt my own son?"

"And why would I hurt him?"

A shiver went through Helen's body, and she didn't leave until half an hour later, when she couldn't cry anymore. "You must fix him," she said. "You owe me that."

"But you don't think that I'm doing God's work."

Helen gave her a hard, sober, stare, even if her eyes were red and her lids swollen. "You think I care. You must fix my son, you owe me."

That Saturday, she went eastward toward the Texas border with Xerxes and Shibuya in the backseat. It was five o'clock in the morning and she listened for the pain to return, expected it every minute. What would she do on New Mexico 88 if she had an attack now and couldn't drive anymore? At home, Carl was still asleep. She hadn't left him a note.

The road led her through more and more nothing. Then a dairy farm appeared and was gone. A small spattering of houses turned out to be Demit. She hadn't heard of it before. She had no idea where exactly she was heading and if she was still on the right road.

After half an hour what had once been a vast lake appeared to her right, a blinding expanse of sand and salt. She turned off the road onto a sandy path, nearly clogged by its collection of tumbleweed. She crawled along, scraping the undercarriage and wing mirrors and doors until fifteen minutes later fences blocked her path.

The information box that had been installed at one corner of the small parking lot contained an empty Allsup's styrofoam cup and a burrito wrapper. She let the dogs loose and hiked down and toward the whiteness. Dunes and dunes and dunes and no water, the air so dry she could barely swallow. The dogs plowed through it as though it might be snow, half-crazed, jumping and galloping, yapping in strange, high voices. The sun had risen barely over the horizon, and yet she wished for even darker lenses. Sunlight like box cutters perforating her retinas.

And there was no sound, not of cars or trucks, nor of planes or harvesters. And there was no sound other than wind in her ears, the sand brushing her face and hair. She kept walking, past the signs that told her to turn around. This morning, she allowed herself to disregard the signposts. What could they do to her out here? Would the state police arrest her and drag her off to jail? She turned, as though a uniformed figure might be hidden behind the next dune.

No other sound reached her until Shibuya's fur stood up and her ugly bark scratched and tore at the silence. And a dark spot had appeared in front of them, then was gone again, only to re-surface moments later from behind a dune.

It was still far off, but she couldn't tell the distance on this beach, where everything seemed right here and miles away at the same time.

Over the next minutes the spot became slowly larger. What had looked as small as a stray calf rose higher and higher, and Jenny stared, uncertain of where she was and none of the shapes she knew to expect from books and neighbors' tales seemed to fit. At last both dogs screamed at what hurried toward them, yet they didn't advance against the creature. Their teeth were bared and they danced in place, skittish, more fearful than she'd ever seen them. And for a few crazed moments Jenny hoped that police had spotted her and was coming after the trespassing woman with her dogs.

Then the creature in front of her stopped. It was thirty feet away and bigger than a camel should have been, Jenny was certain of it. It was a giant, bald spots covering more of his red body than the fur. Something strapped to his back swayed from side to side. Its jaws came apart in a deafening bray.

Shibuya danced, her snout as ugly as a barracuda's, her teeth had never been so long. Her tail was between her legs, and yet she jumped forward, then retreated. Got up on two legs, half-human she seemed, and barked. Xerxes whined, barked at the apparition. His Mohawk seemed to be made from sharp wire. He didn't look like a dog anymore, he was pure wolf and scared.

Finally Shibuya hurled herself at this apparition and was hit by a hoof and shrieked in pain. The camel brayed again, then turned and galloped away. The light and the sand swallowed it whole, she'd never seen a red one. When she stepped forward to where the beast had stood, she found a skull in the sand. It was bleached white and human.

The vet stitched up the dog's wound, the skull had been cracked, she would survive. The bill canceled the shopping trip to Santa Fe, the new coffee maker, the grill she had wanted to buy for Carl, a trip to LA. She would live, and Jenny doubted Shibuya knew at what cost. She would have given her life to protect Jenny.

That night, the pain in her abdomen returned. She imagined she was giving birth to a baby with disfigured hands and feet and several teeth but only one eye. The hair looked as coarse as the doctor's chest hair.

NINE

For we wrestle not against flesh and blood, but against principalities, against powers, against the rulers of the darkness of this world, against spiritual wickedness in high places.

AT THE STIMWORTHS' ESTATE SALE, the dead people's clothes still hung in the closets the way they had left them, new people rummaging through jackets and shirts and ties. When they were still alive, they'd had a poster in their front window, asking about Obama's birth certificate. The appliances were all original, from the late sixties, the carpet seemingly too. Green, grass green. From the backyard, you had an amazing view west. The record player, a Technics, was like new. An old woman on a cane and in slippers looked for bargains. A middle-aged guy tried on the dead man's jackets, they seemed to fit.

That same weekend, a ranch east of town burned to the ground, the insurance hadn't been paid in two months. The owner wouldn't get a penny.

Jenny didn't tell Carl about the red camel. He liked good stories, apocrypha, but she didn't want to share it with him, not with him. Business at her parlor was slow, the money seemed to keep pace with the crops, drying up and eroding faster each new day.

Garrett arrived one afternoon. She saw him get out of a new car, a small Lexus, a souped-up version. He wore a flannel shirt, loose-fitting jeans, his hair had been buzzed off.

"You're trying a new identity," she said.

"I'm leaving. After what you said. You called me a coward."

She raised an eyebrow. "No," she said. "I said…"

"…I was looking for an excuse to stay."

"A reason to leave. Your words."

"That's a coward."

She didn't answer.

"You're right. I have to leave."

"You got the get-away car."

"You like?" His face moved quickly, twitched with anticipation, then turned rigid, withdrew his obvious joy.

"What can I do for you?" she asked.

He shrugged. "I feel like I need something. A plan. So I know that three or four years down the road I have achieved it."

"I don't deal in goals," she said.

"Am I going to be rich?" He smiled.

"Still on that first question?"

He shook his head. "You think I'm stupid,

right? For not leaving. For coming here today. Right?"

"You think that, it seems."

"You talk like a shrink."

"How would you know?"

"My dad sent me to counseling after Aaron died and then again after my first boyfriend. That shrink showed me porn, tried to make me like tits, big like yours. As though boobs were the point."

"I'm not trying to make you like them."

"But you answer my questions with your own questions."

"You want me to give you an answer."

"What's wrong with that?"

"I am not you."

He pulled off his boots. "At least tell me something. Something that will happen."

She received his foot and wondered if she held a young version of J.D. in her hands. She cradled it, engaging with the realm that was as real as anything yet didn't seem to have an entrance. You just happened to enter it. It was an immaculate conception; you knew you were pregnant without any deed necessary. You just were.

"You'll go abroad," she said. "Italy perhaps. Yes, Italy. You'll be living near Naples, by the coast, a small house. I see a companion."

"I always thought Italy was boring." He sat up straight, pushed his foot into the boot. "Strange choice."

She shrugged, received $20 and watched him step outside and into his new car. The engine burbled, shrieked. Jenny was certain that Garrett, J.D. Hartt's son, could talk himself out of any ticket he might get.

She sat at her table after that, nobody breaking the silence in her office which was spiced with the hum of the water cooler, the hum of the refrigerator, the hum of the air conditioner. Cars went past on Avenue D.

She hadn't even seen Garrett's future. His future was blocked to her, no entrance, no getting in either. His borders were as hard as dry pie crust and she had no teeth. She'd given him Dickie Greenleaf's life.

She had experienced blockages before, a disconnect with people for reasons she could only guess at. But Garrett wouldn't waste his time in Italy if he went. If she had really convinced him to leave. That was real. She was also convinced he needed to leave now. She couldn't enter his sphere, but she received signals from within, whispering noises, static. She couldn't decipher them, but she didn't need to. The pitch told her enough. Like lying in bed as a child and overhearing the humming noises from her parents downstairs. When divorce and alimony and visitation rights had not yet been uttered aloud.

Helen picked her up in the afternoon, and they hardly spoke a word on the way to the hospital. "We can't pay for it," Helen said when she opened the entrance door. "The drought was bad enough, now our own son is eating us alive."

There were two more patients in Jared's room. He had the bed nearest to the window, and he gave a tired smile when he recognized Jenny. His blond hair was greasy, stringy, yet even in this drab room he looked like a prince. An enchanted prince, who didn't know who his father was.

Helen gingerly sat down on one edge of the mattress, Jenny carried a chair to the other side.

"We're going to get you in a few days," Helen said and caressed her son's cheek. Jenny watched mother and son; they almost looked like lovers. And Helen seemed to treat him like royalty, lamented his hair and his pale face.

"Leave us alone," Jenny finally said. Helen turned toward her, her eyes full of hatred.

"It's alright," Jared whispered, and put a hand on his mother's shoulder. "Just for a few minutes."

Helen got up, and Jenny could see how difficult it was for her to get her face under control. "Can I get you something?" she asked her son. Jared shook his head.

A Mexican boy occupied the first bed. Four adults and two children crowded around him and spoke to him in Spanish. Three balloons were tied to his nightstand.

In the middle bed lay a sleeping boy. His arm was hooked up to an IV, maybe he had just come out of surgery. Nobody seemed to care about him.

Jared and Jenny stayed quiet for a short while, without looking at each other. Then Jenny said, "Your mother blames me for your accident. She wants me to heal you."

Jared nodded his head. "Can you do that?"

Jenny watched his face silently. She mustn't give him any hope, but if she refused to try and help him, how far would Helen go to take revenge on her?

"I've never tried before," she simply said.

"Why don't you try it right here and now?" Jared's voice didn't change, his question wasn't meant to push her.

"Not here. Not with all these people around." She sounded like a practiced liar. The sound of her reply frightened her.

"They're going to release me soon," he said.

"I know," Jenny said. "Don't demand too much." She stood up from her chair and, following a sudden impulse, pulled the sheet off his legs.

They looked undamaged, long and tanned. His feet were pale, the middle toes longer than the big ones. Jared had a pretty girl's legs. Jenny put a hand on his knee.

"I can't feel it," he said.

"Don't demand too much," Jenny said again.

"But you did find water."

Jenny stared blankly at him. "Water?"

"If the rig hadn't caved in, we would already have a new well. You found the right spot." His eyes lit up. So that was why Helen had sought out Jenny again.

"You found water?"

"We don't have the money to fix the drill ."

Jenny covered Jared's legs, bent over him and gave him a quick kiss on his forehead. "You shouldn't demand too much."

"You found water." The engine of the tiny car droned, nearly drowning out her voice. Helen didn't let on that she had heard Jenny. Her cell, which she'd put on the dashboard, began to bark.

"As if that could still help us." Helen took the cell and pressed it against her ear. After only a few seconds she let it slip to the floor and hit the accelerator.

"Let me get out," Jenny said after they'd passed Avenue D, and she understood that Helen wouldn't listen to her. Instead she bit her lips and, when they had left the town behind them, forced her asthmatic car to go eighty.

The moment they turned onto the dusty county road, Jenny hit her head. The Geo Metro bucked and shook itself, almost careened out of control. Helen's gaze was turned to the horizon, her eyes didn't blink. Her knuckles were of a yellowish white and she had forgotten to put on her safety belt.

Jenny grabbed the armrest, she hadn't wanted to return to the farm. What would Dan and his sons do to her? She searched her bag for her own phone, gripped it tightly.

"It's not about you," Helen said with contempt. "I'm not going to shoot you down."

"Who is Jared's father?" asked Jenny. She hadn't been aware that the question was still stuck in her head.

"Jesus Christ, that's nobody's business. Take a closer look at his feet next time."

The farm appeared to be consumed by flames. But it was dust stirred up by the seven or eight cars, colored red by the setting sun. Helen didn't pay any mind to cars, trucks, or the men who stood with their guns behind the tailgates. She braked, Jenny was hurled forward, and the next moment Helen had left the car and was running toward the house. Jenny got tangled in her safety belt, hit her head a second time on the door-frame. Laughter followed her all the way to the front door. Helen pulled her inside.

It took a few seconds for Jenny's eyes to adjust to the darkness. Dan, Tim, and Gabe were holding shotguns in their hands. From time to time they peeked through a window.

Helen went into the kitchen and returned with a fourth gun. She put a revolver in Jenny's hand. "Don't pull the trigger out of fear. Only when they come after you and put their hands on you. Then shoot them in the face."

Jenny held the old, heavy weapon in her hands. This one was real, she thought. This wasn't a souvenir, no prop. She feared it more than the men outside, but she wouldn't surrender it.

Nobody inside the house spoke, and no voices reached them from the outside. Then shots were fired, and Jenny found herself lying flat on the floor, without knowing how she had gotten there so fast. The others, too, crouched down. Tim held his elbows in front of his face. His gun lay on the floor.

Engines howled, the cars honked, more shots were fired. Dan shouted, "Stay down."

After a few minutes it was over. Only the dust was still swirling around the house and attacked their faces when they stepped outside. No windows had been shattered, no bullet holes were visible in the stucco. Jenny was still gripping her weapon, pressing it tightly against her chest.

"Nobody is going to buy the farm now," Dan said. "Isn't worth a penny anymore. They don't even have to shoot us."

"What about Hartt? He's still going to buy it."

Dan looked at Jenny, as though he was only now recognizing her. Then he spit in front of him. He tried to get a hold of her revolver, but she dodged him, refused to let go of the gun. "Give me your car keys," she said to Helen.

"You don't even know how to use it," she said, but took the keys from her pocket anyway and handed them to Jenny. "If those guys are waiting for you out there, don't show them the gun. Otherwise they're going to kill you."

She stopped at Burger King, went inside and ordered their weak coffee. Then she said outside on the steps and felt the warm Styrofoam cup in her hands. The sky above her only reluctantly changed its color to blue, and on the horizon, the sun was still fighting for a spot. It would be another hot night.

Only after several minutes did she see the police cruiser on the other side of the highway, parked on the lot of the newly torn down McDonald's. Yellow plastic tape fenced off the area of the old restaurant. And then she detected Carl among the police officers, threw her coffee to the ground and started to run. She blindly glanced at the oncoming cars, didn't even try to slow her steps. She ran, ran towards her husband.

Scott Streeter, the officer whom she had asked about dog boy, opened his arms as though he wanted to catch her. "This place is blocked off," he shouted. "You can't be here."

He was barely visible to Jenny. Her eyes were wet, all objects swimming and distorted. "Carl," she screamed at the top of her lungs. "Carl!" Streeter looked alarmed, his right hand lowered itself toward his holster.

Carl ducked under the yellow tape and patted Streeter's shoulder. "Scott, it's my wife," he said calmly.

He slung his heavy arms around her, and Jenny felt herself grow small and smaller. Felt herself become invisible. "What are you doing here?" he asked and led her to his pick-up. "You look terrible."

She laughed, but her outburst ended in more tears. Despite the heat she suddenly felt cold and regretted having ditched the bad coffee. "I worried about you," she lied. "I saw you with the police."

He laughed quietly. "They haven't arrested me."

"Then what's going on?" She wouldn't tell him about what happened out on Helen's farm, she already knew.

"The construction workers found some bones. They're not sure about the origins. Could be of archaeological interest. Or..." He didn't finish the sentence.

They leaned against the bed of the truck and watched the officers send ten or twelve onlookers home. "It's growing dark," Carl said. "They're not going to get flood lights tonight. They're going to lock down this place." He kissed her hair, and Jenny held on to him until she stopped trembling.

"You really look terrible," he said. It was the first time she detected a new smell on him, but she couldn't describe it, couldn't place it. Carl smelled like a stranger.

TEN

And no marvel; for Satan himself is transformed into an angel of light.

THE MAN MIGHT HAVE BEEN IN HIS FIFTIES, but he looked dried up, walked with a hunch, and she had to help him get his boot off. His truck was an old Chevy, two-tone color, original paint. Bleached and flaking off.

"My name's Victor Nix. I have cancer," he said, before she could even get a good look at his foot.

"What kind?" she said.

"Lungs. It's bad," he added, with something like pride. "The doctor thinks I'll be done here in four weeks."

"Are you scared?"

"No, ma'am, I know what's waiting for me on the other side. But that doesn't mean I'm in a hurry." He smiled, exposing orange-brown teeth, a strange color she'd only ever seen in Querosa.

"And you want to see if you..."

"I want you to do your thing."

She understood from his face. He didn't want to know his future. "I'm a psychic, not a faith healer."

He stared blankly at her, obviously not understanding. "I've heard you've been out at a ranch, praying for water."

She shrank, shivered, felt suddenly hopeless. How many people knew? How many people would follow her every step and call her witch? Would spray-painted threats appear on her windows? Would her car be vandalized and set on fire? "I see the future. I can't heal you."

He slowly got up, shaking his head. Then he stared at his bare foot. "Cain't you try?"

"Sit down," she said. She knew what threshold she was crossing. She knew full well. And maybe she was drunk with the power someone expected her to have. Or maybe she was desperate to work a miracle, so people would look at her in a new light. Be in awe of her instead she afraid of them. Or maybe she anticipated her failure, and wanted to fail quickly and decisively.

"Sit down," she said again, and made him take off his shirt. She sat opposite of him, put her hands on his eyes, then moved them down his body, as if his cancer were a small animal and she were seeking conversation with it.

And when she was done, bruises were covering his chest. He hadn't made a sound, but her throat was sore. She didn't know where the screams had come from, where her anger had come from, but this old man stood up, grabbed his hat off the table and his eyes were watering, and he said, "God bless you, ma'am." And she had to carry his boot after him and close the door of his truck. He gave her two folded hundred-dollar bills.

Back in the confines of her office, she felt small nails in her blood. She stretched and felt like running through the streets of Querosa and taunting everyone who braved the heat and showed up outside. Yet after her elation had worn off, she grew scared. What if her tantrum had worked?

The Asian woman stood in front of her salon, a cigarette in her hand. Once again she didn't have a single customer. She was wearing the same shorts as always, the same flip-flops. The sky did not contain a single cloud.

Jenny crossed the street, nodded toward the woman, who immediately put out her cigarette, smiled, and asked in heavily accented English, "You like a massage?"

"Not today," Jenny said and returned the smile. But the woman didn't seem to have heard her and instead opened the door wide. "Come on in," she said, and Jenny followed her inside.

The lobby was dark, only to their left could Jenny see a small lamp behind a half-open curtain. Behind the curtain also stood the massage table, white sheets spread over it.

"How much is it?" Jenny asked. Her eyes slowly adapted to the darkness. To her right stood a sofa with a rumpled pillow and sleeping bag lying on top. Did the massage therapist sleep here near the entrance? Jenny had expected the usual smell of massage oil and incense, with which salons such as this tried to cover up all bodily odors. Yet the whole building reeked of plywood and paint. Perhaps they were still renovating the interior.

"Forty dollars for half an hour," the massage therapist said. "Sixty for a full hour." This seemed expensive for such a sleepy, provincial town.

"Another time," Jenny said and turned around. Her nose seemed full of wood shavings.

"The Red Ghost. You saw a legend." His office was shabby, his walls full of photographs showing him standing next to people who had signed their names on the prints. Many Jenny didn't recognize, but she did remember Oliver North. J.D.'s smile was faint and proud.

"Camels?"

"The army introduced them twenty or so years before the Civil War. They were bigger and faster than horses." J.D. stood up from behind his cluttered his oak desk. "Could go without water for days." Today he wore a white shirt and ornate bolo tie made from silver and inlaid with semi-precious stones. Jeans and cowboy boots. The pant legs were ironed crisply, no irony came near them.

"Soldiers hated them, though. They wandered off at night, had nasty tempers, and they didn't get along with horses. They had some seventy camels and then the Civil War hit and they sold them off. The rest were just set free. From time to time there were sightings. Some mated."

"I have a skull in my car. It fell off the camel. Something was strapped to its back."

J.D.'s eyebrows arched. "No shit."

In her heels, Jenny was taller than him. His hair combed back too carefully not to be thinning. Carl had taught her how to read the signs. His own hair was full, but he was afraid of baldness, as though it were a contagious disease.

"You parked outside?" He took his cowboy hat, rounded the desk, casually, unhurried, then walked to his office door. "You coming? The last time anyone claimed to have seen the Red Ghost was in 1940." He hadn't even tried to kiss or grab her.

She opened the back of her Subaru, burned her hand on the metal. She fished through re-usable bags, dog leashes and discarded running outfits.

"You take a skull and don't know where you put it?"

"I forgot about it. Shibuya got hit, I needed to go to the vet."

"It's not a good omen to see that camel. A woman got trampled to death once."

She looked under the seats, under the dog blanket that had once promised to keep the upholstery clean.

"It's gone," she said. Her armpits were wet. Her face, she could feel it, was red and sweaty. She looked like a fool to herself.

"It would've been a miracle," he said. He looked suspicious, he didn't believe that she hadn't known about the camels, it was clear. "Have you had lunch?"

"I'm not lying." Her words were sharp. It was 112 degrees.

He grinned now. "Why did you tell my son he should go to Italy?"

"I didn't order him to do anything."

"So you just saw his future?"

She glared at him, found no words that could strengthen her position or convince him, much less eviscerate him.

"You're going to run away again?" he asked. "I'll buy."

The Rancho Grande had decent food if you had relaxed standards. J.D. strode through it as though he owned the place, shaking hands, tipping his wide-brimmed hat, nodding. Jenny thought of Carl, she thought of what people saw when they looked at her and J.D. How often did he take women out for lunch? And what happened to them afterward? Was she part of an established pattern?

"What did Garrett tell you?"

"You know I can't tell you that."

He grunted, looked at the menu the hostess had put in front of him. "The green chile cheeseburger is good."

"Good good, or just okay good?"

"Just good."

"They know you."

"Been here all my life."

"College?"

"Texas Tech."

"This town loves Texas."

He didn't answer her. "What's he supposed to find in Italy?"

She squinted, trying to read his face. Was this a real question or just a sign that she annoyed him? "He's got the money, doesn't he?"

"It'll turn him into a snob. When he comes back, he'll wear make-up and skirts." Before she had a chance to even sigh, he said, "Yeah, I know what you college people think. That's why you leave as soon as you get the chance. Only a few don't. They're no good, that's why they came in the first place. Why did your husband accept the position here?"

"Your son is gay, not stupid."

"Oh, he's plenty of both. Have you seen that car he bought? Now he's looking for tickets to Europe and can't even spell that name."

"Then it would be good for him to go. He'll learn how to spell it."

He looked at her without moving a muscle. And she could feel herself getting closer and closer to him, throwing herself at him as though whatever 'soul' she had, had found its true center of gravity. Her eyes weren't insulted, but unimpressed. J.D. was a few years past his prime, and even back then he hadn't been spectacular. Yet even that made her want him more.

They ordered food, received it, started eating in near silence. "There are people moving into town," she finally offered.

"Oh?"

She gave a shallow laugh. "When I walk the dogs, south of town. The old trailers are suddenly surrounded by cars. I think they killed the dogs that lived out there."

He didn't nod. "See anyone out there?"

"Their license plates were not from here."

"Huh." He seemed to think it over. "Where exactly?"

She described the location, but stammered through most of it, she didn't know the County Road numbers or names.

He finally interrupted. "Did you know we hire South Africans on the dairies in summer?"

She shook her head. "They live out there?"

"Not them. No. I'll have a word with Steve."

She raised her eyebrows.

"The Chief of Police. He ought to know.

Jenny stayed silent for a moment. Should she trust J.D. and tell him what had happened to Helen and her family? What good would it do? "They've threatened a friend of mine. Eight cars and pick-ups. They carried guns. My friend refuses to sell her farm."

He ignored her words, hardly let her finish. "Why Italy? California not funky enough?" Maybe he was joking, maybe just masking his anger.

She couldn't tell him, Patricia Highsmith made me do it. "It will be good."

He pressed his lips together, didn't say a word in response. Then he looked for a waiter and said, "Coffee?"

"We can have that at my place," she said.

"You're going to show me your skull?"

Shibuya, her head bandaged, barked and growled, wouldn't be persuaded. And even though it was too hot to be safe, Jenny locked her inside the garage, then started the coffee.

"Your husband out of town?"

She shook her head, she'd made him park his truck at the curb, didn't want the neighbors to see it in her driveway. "He's at the McDonald's construction site. They found a skeleton and some spear points."

He grunted. "If there's more, they'll never finish the new joint by Labor Day."

"The university hopes it's a new dig site."

"The university," he said, then paused. She saw that his boots had worn heels. He saw her gaze. "The most comfortable," he said, nearly apologetically.

"You're a cheapskate." There was no scorn or blame in her voice.

"You're the psychic." He shrugged.

"Yes, don't you forget that." Yet she couldn't see him. His son was difficult, but she found J.D. impossible. Maybe her desire clouded her vision, or maybe he was stronger than her powers. She poured coffee. He drank his black, she added Splenda, her tiny addiction. Maybe cancer was in her future because of it.

She led him to the sunroom, Xerxes and Diesel only vaguely interested in the visitor. The eight windows looked out on the garden and the back alley, and light stole away all colors, everything transparent pus.

She didn't know what to wait for, the anticipation she'd felt when she'd parked in the bank's lot had grown hard, brittle, and yet she didn't want him to leave with just coffee.

He sat down in one of the lawn chairs they'd put in this room, and she took off her dress, her panties, her bra. She hoped the garden wall made from cinderblock would be high enough for the neighbors not to get interested, and anyway, it was impossible to peek into a room when standing in hot daylight.

Still, he didn't move. At least he's no longer sipping his coffee, she thought. She stood in front of him, her armpits wet, her pussy half shaved, her toenails in need of new polish.

He put away the cup, set it down on the captain's table Carl had bought in Los Angeles. His eyes didn't seem to change, no perspiration appeared on his upper lip.

The air was getting thin for Jenny. How long could she offer before accepting rejection? She stared at J.D., a drop of sweat sliding down the side of her body. She could feel it, and he got out of the chair and on his knees and when the drop reached her hip he licked it off.

ELEVEN

And when the thousand years are expired, Satan shall be loosed out of his prison, and shall go out to deceive the nations which are in the four quarters of the earth, Gog and Magog, to gather them together to battle: the number of whom is as the sand of the sea. And they went up on the breadth of the earth, and compassed the camp of the saints about, and the beloved city: and fire came down from God out of heaven, and devoured them. And the devil that deceived them was cast into the lake of fire and brimstone, where the beast and the false prophet are, and shall be tormented day and night for ever and ever.

WHEN CARL WAS DONE WITH HER he was ready to talk. He had not noticed the small bruises, he had not commented on red streaks across her abdomen. He had received what he'd come for, now he wanted her to listen. "It's a mess," he sighed. "But the Clovis points are real."

"And the skeleton?"

"Too recent. It has the police chief worried."

"How recent?"

"He's looking into it. Might not be older than a few years. It's a dig and a crime scene now. The restaurant owner is livid."

"How long will you be involved?"

"We have to dig carefully, in case it turns out to be something significant. The placement is all wrong, though. As if somebody had buried stolen artifacts just for us to find. Still."

"For you to find?"

"Emptied a bag of points and put some sand over it. All the workers will be interviewed. We're asking museums if points have been stolen."

She touched his chest with a sense of regret. His skin was taut, such a baby he was, her beautiful Carl. J.D. was hers, Carl an undeserved dessert. He'd never be the main course, she was certain of that now, and there was no need to upset Carl, no need yet to alert him. The ties were frayed, J.D. had done his damage. Another month and she might pack a suitcase.

Garrett would move to Italy and she would be free to openly belong to her new lover. She felt possessed. She was hungry for cold cuts. She could hear the dogs outside the window greeting the boy in the Superman shirt in hushed voices.

It wasn't in the paper, but the rumors found their way even to her. In her parlor she learned that two homes had been burglarized. "And they weren't insured," Helen, with her six toes on each foot, told her.

Helen's reappearance had surprised Jenny. She knew she was going to see her again, but Helen remained her client, paid, asked to see the future. She didn't mention Jared again. "Will I get money from Toyota or Nissan?" She was flirtatious, she wanted fate to give her a car manufacturing plant.

"Is Hartt making you offers?"

"Not any new ones. He knows we're drowning."

Jenny's fingers prodded the toes, stubborn babies, a too-large litter, repulsive and desirable, a clear way into Helen's bubble, the future in all caps. Yet nothing extraordinary. She couldn't see a new car plant, new riches, new catastrophes. Nothing monumental on the New Mexico horizon, nothing to satisfy the searching gaze. And still, Jenny worried about Helen and her foot. She felt as though this woman could summon forces that might make the future disappear, whisk it away by a force she wasn't able to detect. Or maybe Helen just wanted to make sure that she wouldn't disappear without her permission. Jenny had the distinct feeling of looking at a quiet painting covering an original of far more disturbing content.

"Their cattle are dying, they'll have to sell. Stole machinery as well. They hit where it hurts. They knew what they were after. We're not leaving the house unattended anymore. Can't afford to guard it, really, but there's nothing we can do. We just have to wait."

"How long?"

"Until the end of November. Then we'll be completely broke. All our credit cards will be maxed out."

Jenny nodded, what could she possibly say?

'Pray for Rain' spread on cars' bumpers, on posters around town, at the ballpark, even on campus. Two billboards at the town's entrance and exit, normally devoted to welcoming travelers, begged for assistance in moving God to let it rain.

The second week of September, a rancher took one of his shotguns, killed his three kids, his wife, and himself. Dog boy came through the doggy door at night now and slept in the sunroom. Jenny kept the door to the living room locked after she found out. She feared waking up to Haag's stare. She feared that Carl might find the boy and scare him off. For the first time she felt the urge to give him a real name, dog boy seemed unkind. She was ashamed she hadn't done so earlier. She nearly woke him and chased him off. Haag was not a possibility. Haag was a sound in his throat, some pagan curse. She surprised him with a plate of food in the morning. He stayed and ate, he didn't share with the dogs.

On impulse, she held out a slice of chicken and called him. He cocked his head and came slowly toward her, grabbed the chicken and did not retreat. He was waiting for more.

Little by little, she made him follow her through the living room, the dining room, Carl's office. Each time he entered a new space his eyes widened and scanned everything rapidly. His nostrils flared.

Inside the garage, she opened the back door of her car and put the clear plastic tub with the rest of the chicken on the seat. Two minutes passed, before he put his head inside the car. He'd been around them for years, but was it possible he'd never ridden in one?

Jenny watched him crawl onto the seat and take hold of the meat. She closed the door as softly as that was possible on an old Subaru, then slid into the driver's seat.

The garage door made him cough and jump from window to window. He trembled, dropped the chicken slices and put his hands against the door. But Jenny had activated the child locks. He was trapped.

His hand found her hair and pulled. She slapped him and he howled, cowered in a corner of the backseat, then howled again. The drive to the Baptist Children's Home was only half a mile, and her ears were ringing when she pulled up in front of the office building. She left the car, locked the doors.

Inside, a woman with short, silver hair and glasses came to greet her. The moment Jenny realized it was Delores Price, she felt depleted. She smelled of rotisserie-flavored chicken, still wore workout pants and a shirt Shibuya had repeatedly bitten and torn.

"I have a child in the car," she said.

"You don't have children," Delores said. She looked benign and serene, a lesser saint.

"I found him, he needs a home."

"And you are his guardian?" If she enjoyed the situation, Delores did not let on. This was her turf, there was no need to be angry. A big cross hung in the office behind her, she was God's secretary. "Every child we take must meet some requirements. First of all, it must be willing to come to the New Mexico Baptist Children's Home and participate in the program."

"He's willing alright," Jenny said. "But he's not like other children."

"If he is suicidal, psychotic, or emotionally disturbed and in need of psychiatric hospitalization, we can't help you."

"Somebody needs to help him."

"It seems somebody already is. But let me ask you again, are you his legal guardian?"

"He's homeless. This is a children's home." Jenny's voice didn't have enough air to breathe, she could hear herself squeak.

"You might have to go to the police." Delores' demeanor was still serene, her voice barely above a whisper. A tiny smile pulled at her thin lips and at the corners of her eyes.

She walked past Jenny to the entrance door, pushed it open and looked at the Subaru. The driver's door stood open, Haag was gone.

"Oh, dear," Delores said and went back inside.

Of course a car's door didn't stay locked when you pulled from the inside. How could she have overlooked that simple fact? Jenny stood in the

Children's Home driveway, aware of her body as though she were still standing in front of Delores Price and taking off her clothes. Her own failure, a simple, stupid mistake, amplified the noises around her. A souped-up truck with truck nuts went by, there were voices of birds she couldn't see. Across from the Children's home, four or five horses and several cows stood in a pasture. Everybody was chewing.

Haag did not return to her yard that evening.

The next morning she drove to Victor Nix's pawn shop. A big sign mounted on top of the roof read "SOS Sale," and the old warehouse also served as the local U-Haul rental. From the dusty and broken parking lot she expected to find the store in shambles, with a broken air conditioner, untidy heaps of half-broken items, some gold watches in a grimy showcase and loads of guns. But Victor's place was clean and cool, the merchandise neatly arranged. No dirt, and musical instruments, small furniture, and garden tools had their own sections.

She found Victor on the floor, stacking garden hoses that were still wrapped in plastic. When he saw her, he got up as quickly as he could and took off his hat. "Still here, ma'am," he said.

"How are you feeling?"

"Haven't coughed up blood since I saw you."

She smiled. Her heart was racing, she hadn't

even had the good sense to google lung cancer. But no coughing had to be a good sign. "You have a backroom here?" And when she saw his worried face, she added. "Won't cost you a dime."

He shook his head. "Can't take the money with me anyway. But for a second I thought..." He laughed half-pleased, half-embarrassed. "My heart ain't what it used to be either."

The backroom was a mess, the store's mind. It was here that the broken or yet-to-be-repaired items were left in limbo. Several refrigerators, power tools, boom boxes, bikes. Victor pulled a chair and unbuttoned his shirt. She ran her hands over his back, over the dry, reddened skin of his chest. Somewhere inside was her enemy, somewhere underneath the protruding ribs Victor was eaten like wood was being eaten by termites. She imagined the larvae, the fast and greedy workers carrying mud to keep working and eating. She dug her nails into Victor's skin.

She had never seen a man pass out before.

The moment she got in the door she screamed. The dogs came running, jumped up at her, licked her face, and she pushed them away, lowered herself to the ground, the cool tile doing nothing to ease what happened in her uterus. Shibuya licked her ear and cheeks and lips, and she couldn't fend her off anymore. She could barely moan, no air would fill her lungs. Her phone was still in the car, Carl wouldn't be home until late. She saw Victor's slack face in front of her and wondered if she had taken on his pain, his cancer. Whatever she was trying to prove by tormenting him, did she shorten her own life in exchange for his health? And wasn't it insanity to think she had those powers? Hubris and in-sanity? But when she'd left him, he had thanked her. He hadn't coughed in days.

She stayed in bed the next day, didn't even both-er to drive by her store and tape a notice to the door. Querosa could survive one day without a future. It had done so for an eternity now. But the following morning, she put on shorts and a tank top and took Diesel on her run, and left Shibuya whining and screaming in the garage. She detested Diesel, Carl's dog, and yet he was the fiercest and he would keep her safe. After half a mile the town had disappeared behind her, beyond that one wave of a hill cresting at the Baptist Children's Home.

Pickups came her way, the cabins crowd-ed with men. Even the pastor from the church across the street drove a truck. Then four cars followed in short order, packed with more men. She heard whistling, an empty beer can landed at her feet, laughter sawed at the quiet around her. They had out-of-state plates, all four of them. Diesel sharply barked at them and Jenny was grateful for his antics for once.

It was poor judgment, she knew it, but she still turned right at the Stop sign, then left after half a mile and ran south toward the once abandoned trailers.

A bonfire was still smoking in front of them, despite strict orders against open fires of any kind. Nine more cars and trucks were parked in front of the hastily patched-up structures. Diesel grew nervous, his head turning this way and that rapidly now, a high growl accompanying his movements, a sound like that of a large bird. There was a dog chained to one of the trees out front, his body slack, not reacting to the approaching runners.

When they were only twenty yards away, the dog raised his head and the Superman shirt was gone, his shorts too. The chain was a steel cable, fastened around his neck with a piece of metal and two bolts and hex nuts. The skin underneath was gone, the blood not crusty yet. Bruises covered the body, and Haag seemed to recognize her. He jumped up and toward her, only to suddenly retreat when the cable cut into his neck.

She had nothing on her to cut him loose. Diesel danced in place he was so riled up, nervous.

"What do you think you're doing?" A man came from behind a trailer, carrying a gun in his two hands. Had he been on Helen's farm that afternoon, did he remember her? His face told her nothing, yet she could still hear the echo of gunshots.

Jenny pulled Diesel away, started to run. The dog responded and pulled hard on his leash. She grabbed her phone from the back pocket, punched 911. She could hear the engine of a truck being fired up, the exhaust exploding in curses. She ran through a trash-filled ditch, helped Diesel duck underneath the barbed wire, then followed. Then ran, tears blurring her sight, and she finally let go of the leash, praying Diesel wouldn't run off and leave her behind, and now the sun was starting to heat her skin and finally she got reception and she stammered about what she had seen and now was in the middle of the field. To her left, she could see a truck and two cars driving at high speed along—what road was it? What number did this county road carry?

"...at the end of Avenue I, if you follow that road south."

She let herself fall to the ground, stretched out flat, getting lost in the grass, thirty feet away from an irrigation arm, she could smell the water as though it might rain. Diesel came and pawed her, sniffed her shorts.

She couldn't get the voice on the other end to share her breathlessness, it remained stubbornly sober, as though programmed. She couldn't give better directions, could only give that voice her number, her name. But her number was still Los Angeles, her name unknown, her voice a mess.

"Go down, down," she pleaded with Diesel. She pulled at his collar, wrestled him to the ground. He enjoyed the unexpected tenderness, pressed his head against her belly, half-closed his eyes enraptured.

But a bird flying overhead made him jump up and bark and he didn't stop when a bullet hit him. He barked louder and blood was mixing with his slobber. Jenny crawled away from him through the grass and dirt and then suddenly the barking died and she didn't look back, just crawled, waiting for the sound of sirens maybe, waiting for a bullet to find and quieten her too.

The police found Diesel's body and dog boy was gone, the cable was gone, the story couldn't be corroborated. Had she known she was trespassing? Had she seen the attackers shooting? Could she describe the man with the gun?

The officers searched the premises, but the men living in Yucca Lows were here legally, here to help at the peanut plant, working from sunrise to sundown. Had she taken a picture of the boy with her phone? Was she sure it hadn't been a dog?

The worst part was that she understood the suspicious faces of the police, she understood how improbable her story was. Yet Diesel was dead, and Carl looked at her in a new way, as though he suspected she might have shot the dog herself. He said he believed her and her scraped knees and thighs spoke volumes, and yet it was his dog who had died, the one she had never learned to love. In the evening he got into his truck and after half an hour returned. "How can they live there?" he said, and new concern was in his face and voice. "Who would hire them?"

TWELVE

And the angel thrust in his sickle into the earth, and gathered the vine of the earth, and cast it into the great winepress of the wrath of God.

TWO DAYS LATER, the last week of September, Jenny flew to Los Angeles. A friend of hers, Staise, would have surgery to get lip implants. They'd stay together in a hotel off Sunset Boulevard.

Haag had not reappeared, she hadn't seen Garrett or J.D. She thought about not returning to Querosa. She didn't need Carl, wasn't sure she wanted him in Querosa. They might be happy in Southern California, Amherst, Massachusetts, or maybe Tampa, Florida. In LA, she could look for an apartment for herself.

Jenny arrived at night, and the air smelled all different, the cab's window was open and the breeze hit her face and she was all giddy and wished the drive wouldn't end, only that her back was all numb from the plane flight. From the window of her hotel room she could catch a glimpse of the city's grid and it looked tranquil, but when she stepped out onto the balcony, there was anger crackling in the night air, it was all unrest. In front of the hotel stood palm trees and though it was near midnight, it hadn't cooled off. The drought was wreaking havoc here too, but she couldn't tell from the looks of the gardens, the bright bushes and hedges.

Staise's dad, who lived in Calabasas, was paying for the hotel and for the implants, Jenny only had to pay for her ticket. Staise was restless and didn't want to leave the hotel, so they got room service and watched the palm trees from the balcony. Sirens started wailing and died again in the distance and two choppers circled not far from them, beams searching the ground. Staise was several inches taller than Jenny, a nervous beauty with large eyes and a corrected nose. She was skinny, her breasts ample and enhanced. She was an entertainment lawyer, but she'd taken a leave the previous year and still hadn't made up her mind if she would return. She wanted a husband and a house in Studio City or Sherman Oaks, she wanted kids and two dachshunds, and she was 39 and her savings were gone. She had a crush on Josh Brolin, who'd been her client, she needed new lips.

The next morning they took a cab to the clinic. Staise held Jenny's hand and smiled, she was excited and at the same time her hands were cold and she hardly seemed to breathe. The clinic wasn't the gleaming, sparkling building Jenny expected, with art work hanging and standing everywhere. It was on the second floor of a strip mall, downstairs were boutiques and a sushi restaurant. The waiting area tried hard to look upscale, but the lights were cheaply fluorescent, and the glossy magazines were from the previous year. The receptionist had fake breasts and looked like a white Janet Jackson.

The doctor was a burly guy with a middle-eastern accent, bad skin and thick glasses. He led them into what looked like a living room and showed them the implants, which resembled two see-through worms. Staise didn't want anyone to know what she was up to, she'd told only Jenny and her dad, and she would need time to recover. She had arranged everything in advance and an hour after they'd entered the office, Staise was being worked on somewhere beyond that living room while Jenny read last year's May issue of a magazine for vegans, a yoga magazine, and *Runner's World.*

Staise was done after four hours and they went directly to the hotel. "Only foods you can eat with a straw," Jenny read from a pamphlet. Staise hit her playfully. "Don't make me laugh," she hissed between her teeth.

Staise was in and out all afternoon, and Jenny went to a coffee shop near Vine, and Giovanni Ribisi walked by with two Boston terriers, and David Carradine walked by, and Ben McKenzie bought a latté for a girl who wore enormous shades and had wide hips.

Jenny drank a second Cappuccino. Michael Rappaport walked by with his kids, and Tim Roth parked at the curb, jumped out and carried a Nikon with a gigantic zoom lens. A woman Jenny didn't recognize was with him.

She meant to call Carl, but the thought of Querosa seemed absurd. There was no dog hair on her clothes, she could see no NObama stickers anywhere, no eighty-year-old cowgirls. She thought of calling J.D. but she was in Los Angeles, and J.D. appeared to be a phantom. Instead she walked back to the hotel. Staise was watching an episode of Southland and Ben McKenzie was telling a woman in a diner to try the fish sandwich.

Staise's mouth looked as though she were a fish forming an "O." It was enormous, and she told Jenny through clenched teeth not to touch it. A bottle of Tylenol 3 and a bottle of Percocet lay next to her on the bed.

In the morning they rented a car, a Mustang, and drove out to Santa Monica Pier. It was foggy, and Staise drank her second smoothie and then needed a bathroom and they stared at the sea, what they could see of it, and it was just there. It didn't do much. A few surfers were hanging in the water, waiting.

They took a ride on the Ferris Wheel, and the ocean was still hanging there, only they saw a bit more of it, and afterward they drove to Beverly Hills and Jenny had a sandwich at a small Italian place on Canyon Drive and Staise drank coffee and popped more Tylenol. They went to Hollywood and walked along Sunset Boulevard and Hollywood Boulevard, and Staise thought she saw Sam Neill, and Jenny spotted Kyra Sedgwick and they went back to the hotel. Staise was in a haze and didn't say anything, because she feared her lips would pop.

The swelling of Staise's lips receded after two days, and after four, they went to the doctor's office, and the doctor seemed satisfied, and told them the wound was healing well. They went to the beach and Staise wanted to tan, so they stayed for three hours and Jenny watched bodybuilders working out at the beach gym. Later she shopped for souvenirs along the promenade and bought a t-shirt with surfboards on it for Carl and one with Arnold Schwarzenegger on it. The store sold Superman shirts and she stared at them, and tried to get a hold of their meaning. She almost bought one for herself.

They showered at their hotel and then visited a gallery in Beverly Hills, where a show by a Japanese sculptor was opening. Jenny hadn't heard of him, but Staise said it would be fun. Sculptures of giant flowers stood in the exhibition room and there was white wine and flat and sparkly water, and Gwyneth Paltrow was there with her kids, and the price lists didn't have any prices printed on them, and Staise said she loved the art. Afterwards they went to the Grove and watched a Jason Statham movie and then Staise bought sneakers at Nike and they bought lattés at Barnes and Noble and sat outside and watched the tram go by.

"Where do you live now?" Staise asked. She was drinking with her teeth rather than her lips. They still felt huge and numb, she said.

"Over there." Jenny pointed eastward.

"Too bad you married an academic."

Jenny nodded.

"What is he doing there?"

"Excavating a McDonald's."

Staise made an angry face because she didn't want to laugh.

"They found a skeleton and spear points."

"How is the yoga?"

"There is no yoga studio in Querosa."

"No yoga?"

Jenny shook her head.

"How can you stand it?" Staise said, and then she fell quiet.

They went to the Apple store, and Jenny bought a cover for Staise's iPhone and Staise said it was so pretty, and back at the hotel they watched a re-run of *The Shield*.

The next morning they drove to the airport and Staise got teary-eyed and said, "Thanks for coming. I had a wonderful time." Then she added in a serious whisper, "How do I look?" She leaned in close, closed her eyes and waited for Jenny's verdict.

She said, "Like a kissing fish."

"Is that good?"

"It's great," Jenny said.

"I look terrible, don't I?"

She shook her head. "No, it's really great." After four hours she landed in Albuquerque.

Thirteen

And the angels which kept not their first estate, but left their own habitation, he hath reserved in everlasting chains under darkness unto the judgment of the great day.

IN THE MORNING HE WAS BACK IN THE DOG ROOM, as though he'd sensed her return. She considered driving him to the hospital, to the police. She needed to, she told herself, it was her duty, his presence would convince everyone that her story was true.

She didn't. He never spoke, he wouldn't testify in court. Instead, Jenny took hot water and washcloths and set them down in front of him. She fed him smoked turkey sausage, inspected his wounds, cleaned them with peroxide, wrapped his neck in light gauze. She didn't love him. She felt pity, and not enough to take him to her bedroom and make him sleep there. He was no more than Diesel to her, a beautiful creature she couldn't care for; she didn't feel enough to make him hers. But she wouldn't be cruel.

He wore a pair of shorts, not the ones he'd worn before, and she didn't take them off, she didn't want to know the extent of the men's depravity. It wasn't her problem, she needed her energy for her own life, she couldn't take on Haag's.

But she let him stay in the room and fed him in the afternoon with Xerxes and Shibuya. He drank with them from one bowl, and like family, they stretched out next to one another afterward.

"They're running people out of town," Carl said the next day. He'd asked workers at the McDonald's dig, McDig they called it in the paper, and by now it seemed clear that the artifacts had been planted, and they kept digging only to ensure that no others would be overlooked. Where they came from had not yet been established. None had been reported missing. The corpse had not been placed yet either, and it was the police who kept the site closed off.

Jenny led him to the door of the sunroom, but Haag had left, her evidence was gone. She wanted to forget about the incident, but Carl was done talking about the site and he took Diesel's absence hard.

"They run people out of town," he repeated. "At least that's the rumor. They're buying up large swaths of land. They think a car company might move to Querosa."

"They?"

He shrugged, she could see the discomfort on his face. "Somebody in town has a lot of money to buy the abandoned properties." His mouth kept opening afterward, but no words came.

"They said who it was, right?"

"It's rumors."

"Who?"

"Hartt."

She knew it was true the moment she heard it, she didn't need to be a psychic to know. It made sense, the straightforward solution. And she had told him about the trailers and he had known and not confided in her. He didn't need to, he was J.D. Hartt, he didn't upset his conscience.

"You've seen the trailers?"

Carl nodded. He felt guilty, she could see it. "It's like everywhere else."

"Poverty."

"It doesn't mean it's evil."

"That thirty men live in the remains of decrepit trailers? They're patching holes, but they're not fixing them up, they're not here to stay."

He squirmed. "We don't know what that means."

"They could have killed me, they wanted to."

He didn't answer immediately. "You did something stupid, you trespassed, you know people have guns."

"Why do you take their side? They killed your dog. They mistreated a boy."

"You killed my dog. If you thought these men were thugs, why did you go?"

She failed to answer. Why had she? She had known full well how dangerous it was to venture out alone and tick off the wrong people. That had been true in LA, where people kept handguns in the glove compartments of their Mercedes and Bugattis. So why?

She turned away, the sure way to make Carl feel guilty. She locked herself in her room and thought about what she had wanted to happen that morning a week or ten days ago.

She had wanted Diesel to get killed, she was certain of it. She wanted him gone, and there had been no convenient way. But why had she gone to the trailers? She shook her head violently, she could already hear Carl in front of her door, ready to knock and make up, if only for the night. But she needed to give the thought that was building in her mind more time, it was not a good thought, but it was the ugliest she could find and she was ready to believe it. She had known that J.D. was behind the men in the trailers all along, and running out there had been an attempt at being near him, gorging herself on his power.

Was that true? Maybe. What convinced her was the lack of rage she felt over Haag's treatment. She didn't care. She hated to see the boy suffer, and yet she was able to forget, able to make herself not feel much more than an abstract kind of pain, the kind you expected to feel at TV pictures of Darfur.

It was J.D. she wanted, not the boy, and if he employed those men for his purposes, then there was nothing she would do to interfere. It was the ugliest thing she knew about herself, and it comforted her, now that she had discovered it. She opened the door and let Carl do what he needed to make himself feel better.

He was up early, staring through the glass door at the half-naked boy. Maybe it was his scent that warned the boy previously, maybe Haag smelled the cheap aftershave Carl had been using since he'd had the need to shave. Oh Carl, Jenny thought, why do I see you in such a bad light? Why can't I seem to think one good thought about you? Why am I so harsh on you?

He'd been a player of sorts, he'd never been hard-pressed to take a girl home, girls had come to him. All the things that had charmed her, now felt like childish joys. With J.D. in the picture, Carl felt like a cheap toy, a B-flick, a mac-and-cheese pig-out. She wanted more than Carl was or might ever be. And J.D.'s ruthlessness pleased her.

"Does he come every day?"

She nodded. "Almost."

"His neck." The bandage was dirty, had loosened and barely concealed the cuts.

She saw Carl's face flush and his jaw clench tightly. He was strong, she loved to watch his rage. And how badly he was equipped to do anything with it. He put his hand on the door handle.

"Let him sleep. You can't drag him to the police. He'll bite and scratch."

"The men got to him."

"That's not how you want to do it," she said.

And his anger cooled immediately. He turned away, poured the coffee he'd made into a travel mug and left the house.

She visited him at the dig site three hours later. She wore a dress with a deep décolleté, a light dress, and no underwear. She was on her way to J.D.'s ranch, but she had a few minutes, she wanted to see Carl and pity him. She needed to feel depraved to get up her courage. Two police cars were parked at the site, two uniformed cops were watching a police forensics team. Everybody seemed exhausted, the men in the pit wearing towels wrapped around head and neck.

Carl's face brightened when he spotted her and he received the sandwich and soda she'd bought with the smile of a teenage lover, smitten with his own power to conjure up this apparition.

"Anything new?' she asked.

"Shards, your usual coil pottery and scrape stuff. But only a few. We might be done tomorrow."

"And the corpses?"

"Vernal is missing two," Carl said, turning to look at the cops. Vernal was a town twenty minutes south of Querosa. "They found that the cemetery had been vandalized. Those guys," he moved his head in direction of the forensics team, "they won't be back tomorrow. They're trying to get DNA samples from relatives. Might just be an elaborate prank." He pulled her toward his truck, opened the door and hoisted her onto the bench seat. She was all expectation, as if she were already with J.D. As if Carl were an appetizer, and she let him kiss her and move his hands up her thighs and pull back in surprise when he touched the tuft of pubic hair she had carefully left unshaven, then return with greed.

"Later," she said and finally felt miserable enough to jump off the seat and be on her way. "I have to open my office."

He shook his head, his hands still in the air, still searching for her. Greed would always bring him back to her, even after killing something he loved.

She had already left his embrace, when she detected that foreign scent once more. Quickly she slung her arms around Carl's neck, pressed her nose against his neck, his chest. His cheap cologne had almost completely worn off, instead he smelled of something lighter, sweeter. Ginger perhaps. Ginger and lemon. She turned away from him without looking back and walked quickly toward her car.

She drove fast, gravel hitting the underside of her car hard, and in the wing mirrors she saw nothing but dust. Like a dust devil she advanced, maybe he could already see her.

When she arrived, it wasn't J.D. who greeted her. It was a maid, maybe a housekeeper, she didn't know of such people, never had the money to consider them.

"I'd like to see Mr. Hartt," she said, a bit more forceful than intended. Disappointment made her sweat. She wanted him to come out onto the terrace, bolt toward her, or await her impatiently in the bedroom. He wasn't prepared.

"You're early," he said.

She felt kicked in the stomach. "Yes, I am," she said.

A smile flew over his face. "Come with me."

The housekeeper stayed behind as the two climbed stairs to the second floor and he walked ahead to what turned out to be an office. "I'm trying to get some work done," he said, his tone not friendly enough to relax her.

"Am I keeping you?"

"You are."

She had the sense to turn around and walk away, and she was thrilled when his hand found her arm and pulled her back before she reached the door.

"Silly," he said.

She hit him in the face, a reaction she hadn't seen coming. Then they stood and watched each other.

She turned around again, and this time, no hand reached out to save her from humiliation. She walked down the stairs, where the house-keeper appeared with a face devoid of clear signs and held the door for her.

So this was that, she thought, she would have to make do with Carl—and her betrayal lost its shimmer and promise. Now it was no longer adventurous but weighed on her conscience. How pathetic to return home after being rejected by her lover. She hated her dress, her freckles, her sandals, her long feet. She looked altogether too white.

Then she spotted the peacock. Yes, she had heard people talking about it. And here he was, completely white like her. He earned his keep carrying his white tail behind him, yet he didn't fit Querosa, not even here at J.D.'s farm and se-pia-colored atmosphere. His cry was loud and ugly.

"Ma'am."

She turned and there was Garrett, in mock-dirty jeans, flip-flops, and no shirt. He wasn't as buff as she'd expected and looked strange-ly naked, as though he wasn't used to tossing his shirt. His neck and arms were much darker than his torso. "You came to see Dad?"

"You're still here?"

"I didn't know you...you knew him that way."

"Didn't you buy your ticket?"

"You're gussied up."

She laughed. "Am I?"

"You look different than in your office."

"I'm not in my office."

"I'm not going to Italy."

"Why not?"

He shrugged. "Dad thought it was a bad idea. He said Italy sounded boring."

She felt as though J.D. had chosen to battle her, and even though he had only contempt for his son, he would not allow her to influence Garrett's decision. What did he want from Garrett? Why did he want to keep him in Querosa? She turned to look at the peacock one more time and saw him strutting off, pouting perhaps that he wasn't adored anymore.

"Suit yourself," she said coldly. She fished for her car keys and was on her way.

"Did you really see me there?" he asked into her back.

She stopped. She thought for an instant of taking the high road and saving a shred of dignity. Yet Garrett was J.D.'s son, to hell with him. She needed a target, she needed to hit swiftly.

"Your dad is burning farms and killing people. When he thinks of you at all, all he sees is someone humping you and you grinning with joy. That's what his son is, an ass being humped. Not a nice image for him. He'll never respect you."

The car's engine cut off anything said by Garrett after that. She didn't care, she saw his mouth moving, she saw his red face, and she knew that what she'd said was gaining power with every second. The poison spread, and for the first time in minutes she could feel herself breathe. She forced herself to drive slowly, and the boy in the rearview mirror was hooked, she knew, and the slower she disappeared, the deeper the hook went. She had him good.

That night, she read tea leaves. Carl was at the brewpub with colleagues, Xerxes and Shibuya were asleep on the sofa. Shibuya was bored with her, she was missing Diesel, missed harassing her companion. Xerxes was too dignified to give in to her antics.

She felt calm, the calm of depression, a strange clear-headedness. Did she have to tell Carl about her transgression? For the sake of honesty and his health? Would they still be together in a year? In five?

The tea leaves did nothing to reassure her. What she saw was death—not her own, but she was at the heart of it. And Carl was nowhere to be seen, as though he had vanished completely from her life. She was at the center of death, and beyond that darkness she couldn't make out any clear contours.

The doorbell made her come back to the sunroom, where a single lamp gave just enough light to watch the bottom of her cup. Shibuya was up now and at the door, cautious and curious, ready to bark, training her throat with low growls.

"Did you send him away?"

She stepped out onto the roofed concrete slab, closed the door in front of the dog. "Who? Carl?"

He stared at her in what she thought to be a mixture of contempt and hatred. "Garrett. He's gone."

She shrugged. "Why?"

"I saw you talking to him. Now he's gone."

"Do you care?"

She saw that Carl had left the garage door open, exposing bikes, garden tools, bags of dog food, dozens of pairs of old shoes.

"Where'd he go?"

"I didn't tell him anything," she said. "Are we done here?"

He started to laugh. "You're watching too many crime shows. That phrase. Priceless."

"Your men tried to kill me. They killed my dog. Your men are burning down farms. You're buying land to sell it to Honda, Nissan, GM, whoever wants it."

He stepped back, squinted at her. "Who said that?"

"What?"

"That they are my men."

"Everyone knows."

"Go to the police then."

"I'm sure that will help."

"Then stop accusing me."

Now it was her turn to laugh. "You're the big fish here, right? Because you never left to find a bigger pool. You terrorize the Baptists and

Church of Christ people and the ten or twelve businesses that are not yours. What a man you are."

He grabbed her and she pushed him off, and behind her the dogs went berserk, and startled he paused, and she said, "The garage," and when they were inside, and before the door had shut completely, he had ripped her dress and hoisted her onto the hood of her car. It was dark enough to protect them here, among the shoes with their pungent smell and chicken formula holistic food and the unpleasant aftertaste of a too-hot day.

She was his toy, happy to be of service. She was a box of parts, and he assembled her, put her together piece by piece, tested them out, moved them around, he was thorough. He wasn't quick. Folded her in strange angles. He wasn't afraid of his jagged toenails, his gray-haired scrotum. Not afraid to pull her apart or to hurt her if it served his lust. Yet he wasn't mean, just egotistical. Methodical. Every other minute he rearranged her body and found new ways to enter her. He didn't notice she came with the help of her fingers, she was sure he thought it was for show, to turn him on. And when he came, which took him a while, standing up at his age, her triumph felt satisfying and complete.

Garrett was gone. There was no one left to protect J.D. from her advances.

FOURTEEN

And the voice which I heard from heaven spake unto me again, and said, Go and take the little book which is open in the hand of the angel which standeth upon the sea and upon the earth. And I went unto the angel, and said unto him, Give me the little book. And he said unto me, Take it, and eat it up; and it shall make thy belly bitter, but it shall be in thy mouth sweet as honey. And I took the little book out of the angel's hand, and ate it up; and it was in my mouth sweet as honey: and as soon as I had eaten it, my belly was bitter. And he said unto me, Thou must prophesy again before many peoples, and nations, and tongues, and kings.

THE DAYS THAT FOLLOWED were the happiest since a stint at a psychiatric clinic that had severed the last ties she'd had with her family.

Guilt was a common guest, but J.D. was stronger than that. He was stronger than guilt, much stronger. Did it make sense? Not to her, but she reveled in feeling raw, maybe for the first time since her client had died in a car accident she had foreseen. In the mornings she drove out to J.D.s ranch. Whenever Carl was gone at night, she drove out again.

She was careful to keep J.D. surprised. She bought dresses and shoes, lots of shoes. She didn't feel exciting without buying shoes for him. She offered herself, there was no need for underwear and bras, she didn't want them anymore.

What did she love in J.D.? He was handsome enough, but worn, a small step away from being old. He was rich, yet provincial. He was a bad man, at least in a town of sixty churches. He was the rulebook in Querosa, and she abided by him. The bliss of knowing you were rotten.

She didn't want to confess. What good was it to feel rotten to the core only to turn around and trot along the path of weepy sinners hoping to be spared a hundred years of hellfire? She felt no need to confess, but she was weighed down by the house, Carl's job, Xerxes and Shibuya and their need to walk and be fed and petted. Carl was no problem. Just as she had seen it in the tea leaves, he wasn't even there. Had never been there in any meaningful way. That, maybe, had been the successful formula for their marriage – he'd made no real demands. He was a soft drink you chose because it had few calories and was easy on your stomach. Taste neutral, Carl could never be an addiction. A habit, yes.

Now she had the real thing, the maelstrom, the taste of candy and booze and white powder. She didn't want to confess, and she didn't want to explain. She would leave, maybe leave a note.

A clean exit, no teary discussion. You discussed when you were unsure of what needed to be done. When you knew, you acted.

After ten days she was ready for J.D. She wanted a clean break from Carl, and it wouldn't do to foist the dogs on him. Their babies, their small monsters. She couldn't abandon them, leave behind emotional ties that would sap her of energy and make her feel small. She needed to be big and whole for her lover. Her man. That word sounded right. It was so cheesy, so worn and abused.

"My man," she said in a low voice to try it on, and it made her smile. It was a Speedo of a word, and yet it was the right one. It satisfied her.

Carl had been right about the two corpses. Three high school seniors confessed a few days after the forensics team had identified the dead. Querosa sighed with relief. The rumors about J.D. killing people to ransack their properties stopped. High school seniors were welcome perpetrators, young people did stupid and wild things. The spear points had been stolen during dual enrollment classes. Right under Carl's and his colleagues' noses. And they hadn't killed anybody. No harm had been done. People laughed about the affair. Forgotten were the Stimworths and the burglaries and the men in Yucca Lows. High school seniors. The world could be understood again.

On the spur of the moment, she turned to stop by her salon, instead of going to Walmart to buy coffee, milk, and mouthwash. She hadn't been on Avenue D for days.

Helen sat in front of her door. The awning above the entrance offered her a small patch of shade.

"Can I have one too?"

Helen nodded, handed Jenny the pack of cigarettes and her lighter. Jenny didn't unlock her door, just sat down next to Helen on the still hot concrete.

"You've forgotten about us," Helen said.

Jenny shook her head. "You used me."

"Jared is paralyzed because of you."

"But you found water."

"And can't get to it and pump it. What use is such water?"

Jenny faced the woman. She had a harsh, yet pretty face. Jared had inherited that face. But his legs and feet were another matter. "He's J.D.'s son, right? Have you told him that it's his son? Is that the reason why your farm wasn't burnt down?"

Helen stayed silent, sucked on her cigarette.

"Dan doesn't have a clue, does he? He doesn't even have to protect his house, nothing will happen to you." She paused for a moment, then added, "Of course you told him. Right after the thugs came to your farm. He didn't know. That he had the son he'd wished for all that time. But you told him, right? The next day. Or that same night. That's why you're still on the farm."

Helen turned in a split second and pressed her burning cigarette against Jenny's arm. Jenny was too surprised to make a sound. She scrambled to her feet, rubbed her arm and inspected the red wound. In front of the building on the other side of the road stood the Asian woman. She had to have seen everything.

"If you say a word about this, I'll kill you," Helen said. "You'll heal my son, you owe me that. And if you tell Dan..."

The Asian woman waved. It was a small, blurry gesture.

Helen laughed. "Her arm must hurt."

Jenny kept her distance, pressed her hand onto the wound. "I've never seen anyone come to get a massage."

"Of course not, you dumb cow." Helen got to her feet and extinguished her cigarette. "They park their cars behind the building. And then she goes to work on them." Then she pumped her arm. Up and down it went, up and down. Helen laughed.

When she was gone, Jenny ran across the street and opened the door to the massage parlor. The woman was nowhere to be seen. It still smelled of plywood, but not as intensely as before. From the back of the building, Jenny heard a low clatter.

On tiptoes she walked into the massage room, opened the curtain and took a bottle of oil from a small shelf at the foot of the massage table and sniffed the liquid. Ginger and lemon. A grin spread on her face, she could clearly feel it, it hurt. She saw Carl's boyish face in front of her. Pretty Carl, she had underestimated him.

Steps approached the massage room and the next moment, the Asian woman stood before her. "Is it bad?" she asked and pointed at Jenny's arm.

She shook her head. "Not a big deal."

"That woman is evil."

"Yes, she hates me."

"You like the smell?"

Jenny returned the oil bottle to the small shelf. "Yes, it smells very good."

"You want a massage?"

Jenny laughed so hard, it sound like barking. Then she said, "Why the hell not?"

FIFTEEN

For if God spared not the angels that sinned, but cast them down to hell, and delivered them into chains of darkness, to be reserved unto judgment…

SHE GAVE HERSELF TWO DAYS to pack a few of the items that seemed to belong to who she'd become. A carved and painted wooden egg from a Polish monastery a lover once had given her. The amethyst pendant that was the only thing she owned from her grandmother.

There were designer dresses, small indulgences from Prada and Miu Miu, several purses, her Levi's 501s. What she treasured fit into one orange suitcase, the largest of a trio of luggage. There was room to spare.

When it was done in mid-August, she decided to leave the following day, but then she couldn't stand the prospect of sleeping under the same roof with a packed bag. She didn't want to waste the hours, she wanted to be with him.

The light in the kitchen was orange, the inside of a pumpkin. Doors and windows stood open and there was no breeze. She'd always liked the feeling of linoleum on her bare soles.

In college, she'd observed a girl not much younger than herself, who, every morning around ten, started cooking hamburgers. Whenever Jenny had sat at one of the tables in the communal kitchen, she'd been in that girl's presence. Burger Girl she'd called her, and once she'd run into her at a grocery store, at the meat counter. Burger Girl hadn't looked her way.

It was Angus beef, which seemed sentimental.

The kitchen was her pumpkin, and she poured herself some vodka, and it was nice in this house without Carl, just the dogs staring up at her with great expectations, drooling as long as there was a chance she might give them some. She switched on the ceiling fan as soon as she looked for the spare light bulbs.

In LA, she'd often read Carl's books. They were there, in their apartment. They were free, and often interesting. There'd been one about a guy living by himself on a remote island until he threw out his back and couldn't move anymore. He was saved by coincidence, a sailboat arriving a week into his ordeal. She'd loved the story, still felt the man's regret over his untimely departure, the regret of having to share his living space once again just to be safe.

And then there'd been a dissertation by some Harvard guy from the 60s. Just like the first, this hadn't been Carl's field, but of course he'd taken classes in anthropology, and she had liked the vantage point of intruding into a foreign culture and trying to observe it. Of living the lives of the natives without ever belonging. Of living but not really partaking.

She couldn't remember the name of the book, nor the author's name, but he had been doing his fieldwork in Papua New Guinea. There were stories about the village he'd lived in, and also stories of the nearby cities and the white people who owned mines and enforced their self-serving laws.

And he'd recounted the story of an especially brutal white man and his dog, trained to guard against the native population. Trained like Diesel to despise everyone who wasn't white. And so one night, some of the locals exacted revenge. They knew the dog wouldn't let them come near it, but that wasn't necessary. They'd crushed the glass of several light bulbs and mixed it into ground meat. They threw the burger over the fence and ran away. They never had to be afraid of the dog again.

Jenny picked the nice green plates, heated the oil. Rare, she thought.

She placed three on each plate, didn't cut them in bites. Three on each plate, and she carried them into the yard. Xerxes whined with anticipation. There was a shadow in the corner of her eye, she saw it move along the cinder block wall. Haag was looking at her wide-eyed, afraid maybe that she would carry him away to another home. He was wearing a dirty wife-beater.

Then she left.

She drove the two miles to J.D.'s ranch and when she got out of the car, there he was waiting beyond the pool and she didn't have the heart to keep him waiting. The bag could wait, it didn't mind, that stupid thing.

She ran toward him, not too breathlessly to preserve some grace, but she ran and launched herself into his arms and he accepted this gift, her, the death of her dogs, the bag in her car. Without a word from her or his lips, he accepted, she could feel it from one depraved being to the other, and he took her to his bedroom and closed the door, and there wouldn't be time for dinner. They had a night to fill.

The cries of the white peacock woke her, she could feel how sore she was, how heavy and swollen her lids were. She'd be an ugly apparition but a sweet memory, proof that J.D. could still be devastating.

He was already gone, and she used the time to survey her new kingdom. The striped wallpaper, the wooden chests, the mercifully drawn curtains. The bed had a hand-carved headboard, looked ancient. How many Hartts had been born and had died, roaming buffalo and fleet Indian warriors pursuing them? The floor was made from red tile and felt smooth and uneven under her feet. Her feet looked pretty on red tile. The bag.

Now she regretted having left it in the car. What would she wear?

She found her dress at the foot end of the bed, then stood naked in the middle of the bedroom and felt for a guilty conscience. She was happy to feel it, feeble and helpless in some odd spot in the room. Her extended self, she could have pointed at it with one chipped fingernail. It was there, a benign tumor that over time could be extracted. She looked at her dress.

In the mirror she looked rumpled in that happy way that college-age youths seem to have an exclusive right to. She looked even younger than usual, and radiant, at least to herself. She left barefoot.

The staircase wound its way to the hall and she had reached the large front doors and put all her weight against them, when she heard his voice in her back.

"You're leaving?"

She turned, a smile overwhelming her face and setting it ablaze. "I'm just getting my suitcase."

"Your suitcase?" His voice was still gentle, satiated, but the question pierced her and hit a spot she'd thought safe. "Silly," she said, "I need more than one dress."

"For what?"

And she knew. She knew and still couldn't stop herself, as though she needed the maximum pain to go with the ridicule.

"I'm going to live with you."

She felt feeble, she already knew she wasn't welcome, she knew she had misread him. The shame was a hot bath, she could feel her whole body droop.

"How long?" His face mapped her embarrassment, her false reads.

"I left Carl," she said, as though it had been a sacrifice.

"What for?"

She stayed at the Sands Motel that day and the following. On the third day she switched off her phone.

She'd never read the Querosa Post-Examiner, but did it now; it was stacked on the motel's desk every morning, and in the evening the stack was mostly intact.

Twelve pages every day, and she read everything to make the minutes last. She took to vodka, yearned for the moment when she lost feeling in her cheeks and lips. She rubbed them, but there was nothing.

The car was parked outside, and she had no use for it. She washed what she had in her suitcase. The gems of her former life laughed wholeheartedly at her. They had been picked to be enshrined in her new life out on the Hartt ranch. They hated her for it.

Not once did she think about going home.

She read the book of angels. She skipped Finis Joyce's writing, which made no sense and was tethered by fundamentalist beliefs he couldn't and wouldn't question. God had created man, no evolution had occurred. Who was this man with a PhD who was so firm in his beliefs that he could cut a narrow path through the world and ignore what he saw? He was Moses parting the Red Sea for his blind followers, telling them there never had been any water.

She skipped all his reasoning, his flat explanations culled from other fundamentalists' writing, and instead focused on the quoted passages. Yes, she had thought herself to be special. Had she ever dared to see herself as an angel? No, no, no, no, she said out loud. But she did have powers. She did. And Victor Nix was still alive. She felt the urge to walk up to his pawnshop. They could share some Mohawk Vodka, they could laugh at her fury, the bruises she'd left on his body. They could toast to his health.

Did she have a reason to stay in Querosa? She'd called Staise as soon as she'd checked into the Sands. She could fly out to California and stay in Calabasas. Staise had found a man she was thinking about marrying. He was a Born-Again Christian and together they went to bible-studies classes, and she loved his enthusiasm.

He was a few years older than her, balding, and in Import-Export, she couldn't quite explain it.

In LA, she could get surgery before her teratoma would be able to do more damage. Pain was a constant companion now. She ate Percocet, got rid of the taste with more of the cheap vodka. Even her abdomen felt completely numb.

Jenny did not buy the ticket. She read the Querosa paper and Finis Joyce's book, scouring the pages for quotes about angels. No, she wasn't one of them, but the passages soothed her, the King James Version did that with its archaic diction and vocabulary. It seemed to establish order where there was none. It seemed to tell a story, even though when it came to angels in the bible, there were only fragments. They were male, all of them, it seemed. Nothing beyond that could be established with any certainty, the information was scant. Even Joyce seemed to have despaired and was quoting and re-quoting and re-quoting the same few passages again and again.

In the end, his book was evidence of the absence of angels. They were mentioned, but they hadn't appeared to humans often. How they moved or where they lived remained nebulous. She could leave Querosa. She had enough money for gas, food, and maybe for two or three months in California if she maxed out her credit cards.

And yet the world outside Querosa seemed to disappear more and more with every hour she spent at the Sands. She acquired furniture —she placed a statue of J.D. in the corner by her nightstand. She carved Carl from light birch wood and sat him on the microwave. She made clay sculptures of Haag, Diesel, Shibuya, and Xerxes. Haag in his Superman shirt. Beautiful Xerxes with his double coat of fur, dense tufts of which she had found every day on the carpet. High-strung Shibuya, who Carl had called his Princess, and who would only come inside if she offered her a treat.

On the fifth day she found Victor Nix's obituary.

On the sixth day, she drove out north of town, to see the marvel the motel owner and a slew of new guests had been talking about that morning. She had seen the billboard in the paper but she wasn't prepared for its actual size. It obliterated the horizon, it seemed to defy the skies and the heat and the drought. It reminded her of a drive-in theater's screen. The bright red logo took up three-quarters of the space, and in bold letters underneath stood, "Future Site of 4,200 New Jobs. A Better Tomorrow."

Other cars stood parked by the road, as though the sign, despite its size, might vanish any moment. As long as someone was looking it had to be real. More real than rain.

On the ninth day she called Helen. "Hello," she said and listened to the silence on the other end.

"Yes?"

She even made the bed, flattened the duvet with her hands. The statues of J.D. and Carl needed to be wrapped, the back seats needed to be folded. Her shoes, her dresses, everything was in her car. She wouldn't leave a trace in Querosa. She was finally free to go.

She dressed in jeans and a button-down shirt, tied her hair behind her head. She paid her bill, then ate a Whopper meal at Burger King. McDonald's would open in October, she'd read in this morning's paper. The paper had also announced that Querosa would soon welcome a Taco Bell.

She went to the bathroom to brush her teeth. Then she ordered a coffee and sat overlooking the parking lot. She waited for the right light to settle onto the city, miracles didn't happen during lunchtime.

At 4:30 she got behind the wheel, started the car. Her belly was a raging fire, and neither Percocet nor vodka could extinguish the flames. Jenny curled up in her seat, tried not to think of anything.

A souped-up Lexus turned into the parking lot, she couldn't recognize the driver's face behind the tinted windshield. Maybe that face was laughing, laughing at her. Laughing because Italy was so absurdly far away. Jenny shrank into her seat, closed her eyes, closed them so tight she became invisible.

Tumbleweeds ran in families across the road, but the sky was clear, only toward the horizon she could see it turn brown. It wasn't a storm like the ones they had in April or May, this was just wind. Winds. Strong winds. It was 103 degrees.

All the cars stood outside the manufactured home, and as soon as they heard Jenny's car, they stepped into the yard. Gabe, Tim, their father, and finally Helen. Except for Helen, they were all carrying something. Gabe and Tim carried hunting rifles. Dan held a tool in his hand that reminded her of a drill.

The men stepped away from the door. "He's inside waiting for you," Helen said.

Jenny handed Dan her car key and he gave it to Tim, who lowered his gun, got into the Subaru and drove off. She had liked the car, she didn't have any use for it anymore. She was certain that Tim would take it apart or repaint and sell it across the border.

Then Jenny followed Helen into the kitchen. "You're rich now," she said.

Helen laughed. "We sold two days before they signed the deal. We're only here because Hartt hasn't chased us off yet. We're leaving town. But that's none of your business. You needn't be worried."

Jenny nodded. Maybe she'd hoped for a miracle, for mercy where she knew there couldn't be any. Maybe she had expected, against better knowledge, that Dan and Helen would forgive her and reject her sacrifice.

Jared had a blanket over his legs, and looked at her with what she thought was curiosity. His hair was as long and shiny as it had ever been, but his face seemed dull and slightly bloated.

The silence in the kitchen grew dense after the men's boots fell silent at Jenny's back. Helen took a place between her and Jared and waited.

"Can you heal me?" Jared asked in a thin, steady voice.

Jenny nodded.

"You didn't tell anyone you came?" Helen said.

Jenny shook her head. "I won't run."

"Damn right," Dan said behind her, grabbed her right hand and slammed it onto the wooden table. He pressed the drill thing onto the back of her hand. For a second or two she didn't feel anything. But she heard the high, efficient sound and saw the heads of two nails sit in her flesh.

A deep calm settled over her. She knew she was in good hands. They'd be thorough. She was two yards away from Jared.

"I'll work with my left."

She turned to the boy.

"Get up now."

Acknowledgments

Thanks to Nina Bjornsson, Delia and Edward Avila, Anne Mason-Jezek and Andy Mason, Carol and Travis Erwin, Diane Cole, Amanda and Roger Davis Gatchet, and Alexandra Itzi for wine and cigarettes, big hugs, vodka drinks, *Game of Thrones* nights, and music, always music.

Thanks to Michael Gaeb, Markus Hoffmann, and Jane Dykema, for their thoughtful suggestions.

Thanks also to Ruth Thompson and Don Mitchell of Saddle Road Press, for their support and dedication and love.

About the Author

Stefan Kiesbye is the author of four books of fiction. He teaches creative writing at Sonoma State University.